Bitter Water

By Sherri Smith

Copyright 2012 Sherri Smith

Discover other titles by Sherri Smith at
Smashwords.com:

Troubled Water - Book two of this series.

Table of Contents

BITTER WATER

Prologue

Mara Conley stood in the still night. All she heard was the rustling of the leaves along the sidewalk and the creaking of a left over Christmas ornament hanging from a utility pole. She could smell a slight whiff of smoke from someone who had burned his or her leaves earlier in the evening. The moon was not full, but full enough that she could see the shops and the town that she had left eight years ago. She was standing in front of her Mom's beauty shop; she shivered, not knowing if it was from the cool autumn night or because she was back where she started from eight years ago.

There were no lights on in any of the shops, they roll the sidewalks up early in small town USA, and this was one of the smallest. From what she could see, there were several empty storefronts up and down the street, windows boarded up, forlorn looking in the night. Her Mother's shop was still there in the little building with the grand name of Main Street Mall. The front window displayed antiques, which meant Nancy's shop was still there but she couldn't tell if any of the other shops were still open. Well at least Mother's salon is still here, she thought.

Mara wondered how her Mom would react when she showed up at the shop. Was her Dad still alive? She had no way of knowing. The years had slipped by and Mara hadn't kept in contact with anyone from home. She had decided to come home, perhaps to get some questions answered that had been gnawing at her inside. She knew she had to find herself, and the only way to do that was to come home.

She sighed and got back into her little Cavalier. She turned on the heater to take the chill away from her body and sat for a few moments, just thinking of the last time she had been in this little town. This was her hometown and her beginnings. Slowly she drove back to the interstate and then to Springfield to find a room. I'll start fresh in the morning, she thought.

Chapter 1

The next morning dawned bright and Mara's mood lifted just by the fact she had a little sunshine in her day. Cool weather was normal in San Francisco, so her clothing would be right for autumn in Illinois. She loved warm weather in the daytime and cooler weather at night...but not this cool.

Mara showered, standing under the stinging spray to feel the warmth invade her body and loosen the muscles that hadn't relaxed during her restless night. Lathering her medium length brown hair, she tried to let her worries slip away, just as the shampoo was doing. Mara had learned a bit since she went away eight years ago, but she still had a long way to go to recover her emotional stability. This trip home was only the beginning.

Mara walked next door to pick up a quick breakfast and a cup of hot coffee. Sitting down at a table, she picked up a local paper and started browsing through the classified ads. Since you're here and would probably be here for a while, you'd better start looking for a job and a place to stay. She had enough money to last her for a few months. A job wouldn't be too hard; she had good skills and faultless references from her previous employers and her resume was perfect.

Munching on her breakfast, she went through the classified ads. Nothing struck her as the right job for her, but she intended to apply for a state job in Springfield anyway. She was going to find a place to live wherever her job took her, she didn't want to be right in the same town with her parents. She wanted to give herself and them space as she went about searching for the answers she was seeking. Decatur would also be a good place to look for a job and a place to live.

Back at the hotel, she chose an outfit carefully that would complement her tan, brushed on her make up and highlighted her eyes with liner and mascara. She used her make up sparingly, just highlighting the natural tint of her skin and playing up her jade green eyes.

She wasn't beautiful, but she made the most of her assets. She'd learned the hard way on her way up in the world to dress as if you were successful, even if it meant buying clothes at a second hand store and buying a pair of shoes and purse. Mara had left Illiopolis with just a savings from baby-sitting and tips from shampooing hair in her Mom's salon. She came back with skills and a savings account that allowed her to buy her clothes at expensive department stores and she owned more than one pair of shoes and plenty of purses.

She left the keys on the dresser and left her hotel room, and unlocking the door to her little red Cavalier. She had an address book but hardly knew where to start. She wanted to see her best friend first, find out what it was like in her former hometown, and get a feel for the pace and the general atmosphere before she tried to contact her folks.

Looking at her in the rearview mirror she thought, "Well, you are here, stop putting off the unavoidable, and get in gear. She drove out of the parking lot and back to the interstate she had just traveled down the night before.

The air was crisp but warm enough to have the car window cracked to let in some fresh air. She had forgotten the smells she loved and breathed deep the scent of newly harvested cornfields, and the aroma of newly turned black dirt. In the daylight, it was easier to spot some of the landmarks. Mara saw the smokestacks from the ammunition plant and bunkers where the ammo was stored for use in World War II. She didn't stop at the small towns that she encountered on her 20-minute drive back to Illiopolis, she had one goal in mind, and that was to go home. She drove up and down the streets of what used to be her home avoiding the street where she assumed that her parents still lived.

Driving by the small cemetery, she thought about stopping to visit her grandparent's grave, but she decided to leave that for another time. She passed the high school where she had spent four years of being the ugly duckling and wallflower. Mara felt the sharp sting of rejection. I thought I was long past that.

Not surprising, there were no stoplights in town yet. She drove slowly looking for remembered landmarks. Mara passed by the Baptist Church she attended with her parents, the grade school where she had endured her school years, and the park in the middle of town where she used to go and sit. It was her refuge, a place to get away from her Father's stony stares and her Mother's anxious looks. Yes, the bench was still there although there was a new array of playground equipment. Gone was the big metal slide that she used to ride down with a piece of waxed paper under her bottom to make her go faster. What freedom to slide ever so fast down the tall slide and feel the wind tug at her hair. She was happy that it was no longer permed and now if the slide were still there, it would stream out behind her in ripples, instead of it standing on end because of its brittleness and curls.

Parking the car, she walked slowly around the block. She had been right last night, storefronts were empty and neglected, dirty windows and cobwebs and trash cluttered the doorways. It made her sad, she knew the town had suffered because of the one manufacturing plant leaving town and laying off all its workers, and the other surrounding towns suffering from cutbacks and plant closings as well. She wondered what kept people here. Yet she knew, they were afraid of change, and felt secure in their own little world. A world where everyone knew everyone and you could set your clock by the 12:00 whistle. Of course, everyone in a small town always knew others business; nothing remained sacred or secret in this little town of any other for that matter. She wondered what they had said about her when she left eight years ago. No matter, she was back and was a different person. Recognition wasn't a worry. She was no longer the chubby teenager, with outdated clothes and acne on her face. No, she wasn't a perfect 10, she still held some of her weight but had toned up and gotten down to a respectable size 12. She had changed her hair, lightening it just a little to bring out the natural highlights, and had gone to an expert to find out how to play up her few attributes. Mara accepted herself for what she was, and no longer worried about fitting into someone else's idea of what a perfect woman should be. She had learned the hard way; other people were bad enough about pointing out your faults, and you didn't have to pile on your own version.

Mara knew if she asked at one of the business places in town how to contact her one true friend that it would be all over town in a heartbeat. Small towns have their own way of spreading the news, and since her mother was the local beautician, she would know almost immediately that Mara was in town. She couldn't face that just yet. She still wanted and needed to talk to her best friend Heather Gentry. Was she married? Did she have children? What was her life like now? Mara knew she'd still be here. Heather was the type that would never be happy living anywhere else except in her hometown, with her parents and family and even larger circle of friends.

She sat in the car at the edge of the park, wondering just how she would go about looking for Heather. She must be married by now, but which one of her many boyfriends finally won her hand? Still she sat, listening to her favorite Tim McGraw CD and trying to decide where to start. There had to be a way. Illiopolis didn't have a library or local newspaper so she couldn't do research to find her. She knew in her heart Heather would have children by now. Driving over to the grade school and just watching was one of the easiest ways to see if she could spot her. Everyone dropped off and picked their kids up, it was the small town way and she had a feeling Heather could be found here.

Mara parked her car in a shady spot, pulled out a paperback by Pamela Kimmell, her favorite mystery writer, and prepared to wait. Sitting in her car, with the warmth of the fall sun pouring through the windows, the book slid out of her hand and she drifted off to sleep.

Chapter 2

While she dozed, Mara began to dream, the same one she had been having since she had seen the Doctor in July. She was running, running down a hallway, closed doors flanked both sides of her. She heard someone crying but she couldn't find which door to open. The school bell woke her with a start and she looked at the parents that were waiting outside the school. Would she recognize Heather? She hoped so but was unsure of herself. It had been eight years since they had seen each other.

Amazed she sat straight up in her seat. She would recognize that walk anywhere. Heather always had an extra bounce in her step and the same blonde hair, just a little shorter now, she no longer wore it in a ponytail. She was pushing a stroller but Mara couldn't tell how old the baby was or if it was a girl or boy. She waited until Heather had collected a little boy around five, probably from the Kindergarten group that had just come out with their teacher. He had the same blonde hair and a big grin as he ran to his Mother, throwing his arms around her and hugging her tight. Mara's throat tightened and she felt tears forming. How wonderful to have someone love her like that.

Stepping out of the car, she crossed the street in quick strides. "Heather? Please stop for a moment."

Heather turned slowly and broke out in a huge smile. "Mara, I can't believe it's you. I've missed you so much, where have you been? When did you get back? Have you visited your parents yet? Oh,

there is so much to talk about I can hardly wait."
They hugged each other and time slipped away, as
if she had never been gone.

You look great and your children are beautiful."

"Let me introduce you to Joseph Junior, JJ for short,
he is five and little sister Melody is 18 months.
Wait; let me make a phone call." Heather pulled a
cell phone out of the oversized bag that she was
carrying and speed dialed a number.

"Joe, guess what? My friend Mara is in town. Isn't
that great? She is coming home with me so would
you please stop and get some carryout on your way
home. Thanks honey, I'll see you in a couple of
hours. Love you too, bye"

Turning to Mara she said, "Where's your car
parked? You have to follow me home; we live in an
old farmhouse just on the city limits. I can't wait to
catch up on where you've been and how you are."

Mara pointed to the Cavalier and Heather gave her a
little shove toward it. "Get going girlfriend, we have
lots to talk about."

Good old Heather, Mara thought, just as bossy as
ever and just as confident in getting her way.
Smiling she got in her car and started the engine.
Heather had always told her she was beautiful on
the inside as well as the outside, but Mara never
believed her. She just knew that Heather was her
best friend and would always stick up for her when
the other girls tried to put her down.

Following Heather's minivan to the edge of town and trailing her into a large circular drive with the garage sitting just in the back of the house. The house was old, but taken care of, featuring well tended flowerbeds, and the yard neat and manicured. Leaves filled recycle bags and were waiting on the street. A swing and a couple of white rockers occupied the front porch. Heather has great taste. She helped me put the right clothes together, even though I had a limited wardrobe. Two beautiful golden retriever dogs came running around the corner of the house to greet them.

"Oh Heather, these dogs are wonderful. I love dogs and hope to have my own one day."

"They are Rascal and Culprit. I'll tell you how they came about their names someday," Heather laughed. "Seriously, Joe works long hours and the dogs won't let anyone on the property that isn't with one of us. Their darlings and great with the kids"

Following Heather up the front steps, she couldn't help but feel welcome. Her home radiated warmth, comfort, and she felt right at home the minute she stepped in the front door. She gazed around her at the high ceilings, natural woodwork down to the hardwood floors, the color of an old penny but shiny as a new one.

"Mara let me get JJ his snack and put Melody down for her nap so we can talk. Make yourself at home in there and I'll bring us a glass of tea."

Mara walked into the living room and looked around. Seeing pictures on the mantle, she went over to look. She saw Heather as a child, and a young boy that she assumed was Joe as a toddler. Pictures were lined up, of her children and family members. Mara recognized Heather's Mom and Dad, and her older sister Kelly. She came to a wedding picture and picked it up to study it. Joe was handsome, short, and stocky with strong features and curly brown hair. Not someone she would have pictured that Heather would choose, but he had a great smile and you could see the twinkle in his eye. Slowly she set it back down and turned as Heather came through the doorway with two tall glasses of iced tea.

"its sun tea, probably one of the last days of the season we'll have enough sun to make it the right way, so let's enjoy!"

They sat there sipping their tea, studying each other. They were at ease, it didn't matter they hadn't been together for almost eight years. It could have been just yesterday they had last talked.

"Mara, where are you staying? I have a guestroom, I would love to have you here, and I know Joe wouldn't mind. Do you remember Joe, he was two years ahead of us in school, played on the football team that won the championship his senior year. He always had that lop-sided grin and his hair was always in his eyes. The summer after our senior year we ran across each other, and well one date led to another and we were married within a few months"

"Please stay here Mara, even for a few days. I know you won't go to your folk's house. Do they even know you are in town yet? Have you seen them? Are you going to?"

Mara looked out the large picture window. She could see a tire swing hanging in the sycamore tree, a picnic table, and bar-be-que grill. She sensed such a feeling of peace and serenity. She knew she would be comfortable here until she could get on her feet and she was happy to know that their relationship had survived the eight years separation. She thought of the dreary hotel room where she had spent last night.

"If Joe doesn't mind, I would love to, but only until I decide what I am going to do."

"Ok, that's settled then, you are welcome here as long as you need to stay. Joe won't mind at all, he works long hours and will be happy that I will have someone to keep me company when he has to work late. Now, where have you been, and what are you doing back and by the way, you look wonderful. Get ready to tell all, I can't wait to hear about your adventures."

Mara smiled, relaxed in her chair, and began to tell her best friend all that had happened in the last eight years.

Chapter 3

Mara began her story, starting with the first night, she had left, but they didn't get far. The front door opening interrupted her story and the tantalizing smell of fresh baked pizza drifted from a couple of boxes held in Joe's hands.

"Hey sweetheart, I have pizza, is that ok? JJ will love it and I was having a craving for it." He took the pizza boxes into the kitchen and came back to give his wife a hug and a kiss. Joe held her for a few seconds, brushed her hair behind one ear, and kissed her again on the nose.

Joe said, "I knew if I brought pizza home, you wouldn't lecture me on cholesterol levels." He turned and gave a little wink to Mara while Heather laughed.

"You're so bad, do you know that? I love you anyway. I hear JJ stirring in his room, he is playing with his Thomas train table, and Melody is just now waking up from the sounds of the baby monitor. Joe, let me introduce you to my best friend Mara."

Joe held out his hand, "Hi, Joe Davis, I am so happy to meet you; Heather has talked of you for so long. I know she has missed you and I'm glad you're here. We have a crazy household but we have fun. I'm surprised I can get a word in edgewise."

She liked him already, he was funny, but you could tell by his eyes that he was thoughtful and serious. Mara took his outstretched hand and looked him over, approving of what she saw. He had brown hair, sparkling brown eyes, and a smiling face. She was a little surprised to see him in a State Trooper uniform. Heather must lead an interesting life.

"Good to meet you Joe, I love your home and think your children are awesome. I'll be happy to baby-sit for you any time!"

"We could take you up on that, so be careful what you wish for." He replied.

Joe slipped off his holster and stepped over to a hall closet to lock it in a safe on the top-shelf. She already liked him, that one act showed that he cared for his family's well-being and there wouldn't be any gun accidents in their home.

Heather said, "I'll go up and get JJ and Melody and we'll have dinner. The easy way tonight, don't you think Joe? Paper plates are fine with me, and it will be quicker to clear up."

Joe headed for the kitchen, Mara following. She admired the beautiful tile floors, the natural woodwork, and the stairway going upstairs. "This is beautiful Joe did you do all the remodeling work?

"Heather and I worked on it together. We wanted our home to be perfect when JJ arrived, we didn't make it in time," he chuckled.

In the kitchen, Mara looked around and marveled at the modernization. Still the country charm made it warm and welcoming. She especially liked the breakfast nook with windows all around so the sun could flow in. She thought, I would love to have a home like this, so full of light and green plants…and happiness.

"Can I do something to help Joe?" She asked.

"Sure, glasses are in that cupboard right there, ice in the freezer, soda for us and juice for the kids in the fridge. I think there is some salad in the fridge as well, we can have that and at least it will make my meal choice look healthy anyway." Laughing he walked around the kitchen, preparing for their dinner. "We don't eat take out food too often and was surprised when she called asking me to bring home something. She's watching my weight, helping me keep fit and trim for my job."

Mara laughed and went to work getting the glasses filled with ice and soda, and filled a toddler cup for Melody and a small Thomas the Tank Engine for JJ, guessing it was his favorite cup. He had been wearing a Thomas sweatshirt when she had first seen him. Joe was comfortable in the kitchen preparing for their meal. He kept her laughing at the funny stories he told about traffic stops, and stupid criminal acts. He laughed, "You'd be surprised how many felons will leave something behind to lead us right to them."

Joe put the plates out, and prepared napkins and had baby wipes handy so when Heather came downstairs all she had to do was guide JJ to his chair and put Melody in her high chair. Dinner conversation was light and playful with JJ keeping them laughing telling about his day and a 'girl' who kept teasing him.

"Don't worry son, she teases you because she likes you. You'll enjoy the attention in about ten more years." He ran his hand over his son's hair. Melody not wanting all the attention to go to JJ decided to run her fingers, all covered with pizza sauce through her blonde curls. They burst out in laughter; she was such a sight with sauce in her hair and all over her face and a big grin as she clapped her hands. "Drink, drink." She said waving her hands in the air. Heather handed her a toddler cup with handles on both sides and Melody was happy. She was so good-natured and Mara fell in love with her.

Heather stood up, "Come on Melody, we need to clean you up so we can tell you hair is blonde and then into your pajamas for story time. JJ, help Daddy clear the table, your bath will be next."

Mara was in awe, was this what a family is like? This was something she never experienced while living at home with her parents. No conversation at the dinner table, or paper plates, just eating and the evening news on TV. She couldn't believe how close this little family was and she was enjoying every minute of being there. Maybe she would rethink her position on marriage and children. After seeing her parents and the way their marriage worked, she had vowed to never have a child and put them through what she had gone through. This was different, and she loved children, she had always been the most popular baby-sitter in town. She didn't date and was always available in the evenings. Since most of the town brought their kids in for haircuts at her mom's salon, she also knew them well. She had already fallen in love with JJ and Melody; she let the thought cross her mind. I would make a good Mom, I know all the actions not to do, and I love children. Shaking her head, she started up the stairs following the laughter of the children while preparing for bed. Leaving San Francisco has addled my brain.

Chapter 4

The house was quiet now; Mara had enjoyed the bedtime routine, the storybooks, and saying their prayers. Melody had been so cute saying "Mama, Mama, Pray the Lord."

JJ had a long list of blessings he went through, trying to hold off the unavoidable. After prayers, each child received a hug and kiss. Turning a night-light on Heather and Mara left the bedrooms.

They finished clearing the kitchen and had taken a cup of hot cocoa back into the living room and made themselves comfortable in the two recliners. Joe had gone to his office to work on some paperwork and watch a football game on TV, so they were alone.

Heather spoke up first, "Mara, what's going on? You have been gone for eight years; you look as if you have done well. What brings you back? I've missed you so much and prayed for you every day. I'm so happy to have you here, now tell all. I can't wait to catch up with what you've been doing."

Mara reflected on the last few years of her life as she watched the dancing flames in the fireplace. It was warm and cozy, and it had been so long since she had allowed herself to be close to anyone, male or female. She hadn't made close friends at her job in San Francisco, and her one relationship with a man ended before it started. She had too many issues he wasn't able to cope with. He'd made her feel unsure of herself and her skills. Her counselor was assuring her she was strong enough to be alone if needed to be. She knew she wanted a different life, different from her childhood. The biggest reason was the Doctor's diagnosis of an inherited eye disease. Sure, there had been a few recorded cases when the disease showed up after skipping several generations, but those were rare.

"Heather, I have Retinitis Pigmentosa, it is a disease that causes degeneration of the retina. The photoreceptors in the retina that allow us to see eventually degenerate and die. It starts out with tunnel vision and progresses to difficulty seeing at night and then finally blindness. This is a genetic disease and I have to find out which side of the family I inherited it. In case I ever have a child, I would want tested to see if I could pass it on. I don't know of anyone on either side of my parent's family who has had this disease. The Doctor said it could skip generations but it was a rare case. I am puzzled, and I want to find some answers."

Mara continued, "Plus, I need to face my childhood and understand why I am the way I am. My parents are so different, and I want to know where my personality came from, why do I have green eyes when they both have blue? Why did my Father ignore me while I was growing up? My Mother differed to him in everything, and only when we were alone at the shop did she talk to me, or even touch me in anyway. I need answers."

"When are you going to let your parents know you're here? It'll soon get around that Barbara and John's runaway has come back to town. You know how rumors circulate here; nothing has changed in that department at all."

"First my ophthalmologist referred me to a Doctor in Springfield that he knew personally. I'm to go to him so he can keep track of my disease. I'm taking Vitamin A supplements as a trial to see if it will retard the progress of the degeneration. Right now, it isn't bad, just some trouble with tunnel vision. The Doctor caught it early when I started having problems with seeing anything but what was straight ahead of me. He said sometimes a person would get into their 50's or 60's before total blindness."

Heather listened closely to her friend's story. She had known that Mara's childhood was not a happy one. Mara's parents never allowed her to stay overnight anywhere with a friend, or do any activities that were important to kids and teenagers. She remembered one time especially. It was the night of the Football State Championship game, she already had a crush on Joe, and she wanted Mara to go with her on the fan bus. Mara's parents hadn't allowed her to go and she knew Mara cried for days because she missed it, and it only made her more withdrawn at school. She knew that everyone had been there but her from her small school. She missed the game and the victory parade and celebration when the team and fan buses returned home.

"Well I want you to stay here for as long as you want to. You can search for a job and if you decide to move to Springfield or Decatur, then I'll help you settle in. I have some friends in both cities, and Joe knows a few people and the safest neighborhoods."

Mara answered, "You are the best friend ever, and I am so glad you have remained my friend even though we haven't seen each other in eight years. I had to leave town, I took the bus the night of graduation, you remember don't you? You invited me to your graduation party and for once, my parents said yes, that I could spend the night with you. I could hardly believe it, but I packed up my backpack and a small suitcase with as much as I could fill them with and left, just as if I were going to your party. Instead, I hitched a ride to Springfield and caught a bus for as far west as I could go. I had some money saved from baby-sitting and shampooing hair; no one knew what my stash was. I found myself south of Oakland in a little town called San Lorenzo. I knew you thought I couldn't come because my parents wouldn't allow it, and I knew my parents wouldn't expect to see me until the next day. It was the perfect time to go."

Heather nodded her head, "Yes, no one missed you till late the next afternoon. Your Mom called to tell you it was time to come home. That's when we knew you were gone. I think your parents knew you had run away and didn't make out a police report or anything. I cried for days, but I can understand why you needed to go."

Mara continued, "I worked as a waitress at night, took college classes during the day and earned my degree in Public Relations. With that, I took the BART over to the city and started making my rounds. I ended with a temporary service and I enjoyed every day of work. I worked in all different parts of the city, and met so many nice people. Yet, I didn't stay long enough at one job to make any close friends. I didn't do the club scene, or stop for drinks after work, so I spent much of the time alone."

Heather asked, "Did you like living in a big city? Did you get a place there when you started working there? What was it like? I'm so anxious to hear, I've never been to a city bigger then St. Louis and then only to the ballpark. I've always wanted to see the Golden Gate Bridge and ride the cable cars."

"I loved the city, every time I moved to another job, I had another view of the Bay, or Alcatraz Island, or the Golden Gate. It was awesome and I made myself get out and enjoy my time there. I loved China Town, riding on the cable cars and I never tired of going to Baker Beach just to enjoy the water lapping on the shore and the smell of the Bay. I enjoyed concerts at Golden Gate Park and eating my lunch at Ghiradelli Square. I'll miss all of that, but I knew I had to come home."

"You can always go back."

"Yes I can, and I can do that if I choose to return."

Mara stood up, "I know you have to get up early to get Joe and JJ ready for a new day tomorrow, I don't want to keep you awake any longer."

"Let's go get your suitcases out of the car, and I'll show you to the guestroom."

"Yes, I checked out of the Hotel this morning figuring I could always check in again if I couldn't find you or decided I couldn't stay in town."

There's a small bath right off your room, so you'll have your privacy. Sleep as late as you want to in the morning, I'm helping out at JJ's school tomorrow and Melody is visiting her Grandma so you'll have some peace and quiet."

Chapter 5

Mara slept all through the night, unaware of the household getting ready for their day. Stretching, she looked around her and studied the room she would call home for a bit. The sun shone through the miniblinds and lace curtains that were hanging at the window. That window faced the east so she knew if she were up early enough she would see a sunrise over the fields on a frosty morning. The other window overlooked the backyard and pond she had seen from the living room the day before. It was beautiful and the swing set and playhouse made her love it even more. It looked so peaceful. She looked around, patriotic colors decorated her room, and a homemade quilt covered the bed. The effect was elegant but simple and comfortable at the same time. A scent of potpourri was in the air, the hardwood floors shined, and a cozy rag rug lay beside the bed to step out on. The dresser and bureau featured lace doilies and old family pictures. Surprised she picked one up of her and Heather when they were in their freshman year. She remembered the day, it was one of the few good memories she had. Looking at that picture, she couldn't believe that Heather had become a special friend. There was a world of difference between them, Mara's brunette hair always permed, and frizzy, Heather's was long, blonde, silky, and shiny. A pair of baggy jeans with a long top in a vain try to cover her bulges was Mara's usual outfit. Heather, pony tailed with shirt tucked in to a pair of slim jeans, looked great.

Looking at herself in the mirror, she decided she had come a long way from that chubby, shy freshman. She learned how to take care of her skin, tone up her body, and let her hair fall around her shoulders and free of any chemical solutions that would frizz the ends. She felt satisfied with her appearance. Not perfect, but her motto was "I am who I am, God made me this way. I am who I am, I'm just me."

After soaking in the tub with the scented bath salts that Heather had put there for her, she felt like a new person. Unpacking her robe she felt so sure what she was doing was right. She was ready to tackle the day, no matter what it would bring. First, she needed a cup of coffee. She had noticed a Bunn coffeemaker in the kitchen the night before and was sure there would be coffee around. Slipping on her robe and slippers, Mara walked down to the kitchen, she looked at the home that Joe and Heather shared. It had peace and love written all over it. Family pictures, JJ's drawings on the fridge, small little fingerprints on the French windows on both sides of the patio door. She knew much love had gone into remodeling this old home. She felt a twinge of jealousy but then allowed herself to be glad for her friend's happiness and determined that she would absorb as much as she could.

Sure enough, there on the counter was a note:

Mara, hope you had a good nights rest. The coffee is in the cupboard above the pot, sugar, and creamer on the counter if you use them. Also on the other counter, you will see a breadbox; there is bread and bagels with anything you want to put on them in the fridge. Can't find anything? Just look, make yourself at home and I'll see you about 4PM. I'm so happy you're here; I can't wait to talk more tonight.

Love, Heather

P.S. Dinner is in the crock-pot, you don't have to do anything but relax and enjoy.

Mara sat sipping a cup of steaming coffee and munching on a bagel with cinnamon butter, thinking of her day. She wasn't sure where she should start. She thought she would try to see her Mom first and let her break it to her Dad. Anxiety about her welcome caused her stomach to churn with the thought of the ordeal. Squaring her shoulders, she stood up and cleaned her breakfast spot. She rinsed off her dishes and placed them in the dishwasher. Looking out the window, she could see the covered brick patio and summer furniture that hadn't yet been placed in storage. It was a restful sight and gave her fresh determination to find her answers then start a new life for herself. Mara, you didn't come this far to back out now, you can do it.

Unpacking her suitcases and hanging her clothes and putting underwear away in the empty dresser drawers soothed her. She liked her surroundings to be neat and orderly, she knew she learned that from her Mother. Scanning her wardrobe, she decided her clothes would be fine to find a job and work for a while before she had to invest in heavier clothes. Her layered business suits worked just as well here as they did in San Francisco. She knew she needed to buy a good winter coat. This part of the Prairie

State had its share of blizzards, ice storms and below zero temperatures. She remembered those cold black spells, stuck at home with both parents. Those times, when no one could get out because of ice storms, downed power lines and slick roads made her more unhappy. Shake it off Mara, that's in the past and you're a different person now.

Carefully she chose a pair of black dress pants, and a soft lavender sweater and black loafers, hair brushed and shiny, with just a hint of make up, she felt she was ready for whatever the day would bring. Skipping down the stairs, she found her jacket lying on the hall tree bench with a key labeled 'house key.' She smiled, how sweet of her friend to let her know that she would have the run of the place. Getting into the car she was optimistic about her future and knew in her heart she was where God wanted her to be. Apprehensive, yes, but still determined to uncover her past and expose it to the bright sunshine of a new dawn. Only by facing her past, could she have a future. Today would be the start of it.

Chapter 6

Retracing her drive from the afternoon before, she found herself again in front of her Mom's beauty salon. She knew her Mom came in early on Fridays, one of the busiest days of her week. She sat in the car, looking at the storefront of the little place called Main Street Mall, a fancy name for two antique stores, a beauty salon, and an insurance office. At least the windows were clean and there weren't any leaves or debris in the doorway. It was sad to look around at what used to be a thriving business district. The only other buildings still in use were the bank, post office, and a hardware store. She knew the town now had two bars. The bowling alley was gone and a bar now stood there instead. Also, the Catholic Church and the Baptist Church were still in their usual spot. The Baptist Church was where she had gone to Sunday school, Church, Wednesday night services, Sunday night services, and AWANA club on Thursdays. She wasn't allowed to be a Brownie or Girl Scout but she could be active in AWANA, a Bible based program much like the Scout programs. It did give her some contact with kids her own age but that ended when she was 12. That's when she started working in her Mom's salon.

Getting out of her car, and walking to the door, she nearly tripped over a calico cat sitting by the door. She hadn't been able to pick it up because of her vision problems. "That would have made an impressive entrance," she thought. She smiled; she could almost see herself flat on her face and picking herself up off the fake brick floor. She looked around; they had added a couple of new stores in the tiny spaces. One was a tearoom, and the other one was a tanning salon. It looked attached to her Mother's salon and it surprised her. If it was the only tanning booth in town, it had to boost business. She wondered whose idea that had been. Not her Father's she was sure. The idea of tanning nude in a bed of ultraviolet rays would be something her Father would not approve of.

She peeked into the first of the two antique shops. Yes, she could see Nancy was still there, looking the same as she had eight years ago. Time had been good to her; she didn't look 82 years old. She had looked the same way for as long as Mara could remember. She passed it by, she would stop in later, but first she had to see her Mom. She would have to remember to call her Mother, which is what she preferred over Mom.

She hesitated, and then pushed open the door to her Mother's shop. The sharp burning smell of permanent solution assaulted her senses. It was as familiar as the scent of lilacs blooming outside her bedroom window in the spring.

Barbara Conley looked up from what she was doing. The scheduling book and pen went crashing to the floor.

"M-Mara?"

"I'm glad you didn't have a pair of scissors in your hand, you might have a hole in your shoe." Mara didn't know how her Mother would react so she tried the light tone of voice and a forced, but friendly smile.

"What are you doing here? I thought I would never see you again." She stood there in shock then gave Mara a quick hug and stepped away.

Mara noticed many changes both in her Mom and in the Salon. First, she was surprised to see her Mother in a pair of slacks with a smock over her print blouse. Her mother had not even owned a pair of slacks while she was growing up. Mara had begged and pleaded to be able to wear jeans or slacks when she started high school. Catherine's chin length hair feathered her still beautiful face. This was amazing to Mara, who could only remember her long hair, curled and held up by a clip or twisted into a French roll. Was that just a hint of make up around her mother's eyes? She wondered what else she would find changed.

The salon was clean with country curtains covering the bottom half of the windows that looked out to the interior of the mall. A wallpaper border gave the room charm and warmth. A nail booth sat in one corner and a hall tree in the other. Barbara saw her daughter glancing at the nail booth and explained. "I have a woman who comes in two days a week to do nails for my customers. She has an excellent following and she pays me a portion of her earnings as rent. I also added a tanning bed by opening a connecting door to the shop that used to be next door. I needed to raise the income of the shop."

"A perm and a coloring job canceled for this morning, so we may as well go have a cup of coffee since you're here." Together they walked in silence to the tearoom for what Mara hoped would be the beginning of many long talks. Tension filled the air and Mara felt uncomfortable. She thought, this is what you came back to do, and you're going to do it. You need to reunite with your parents and find out some family history. Mara knew it would be hard, what she didn't expect were the feelings of fear and hostility coming from her Mother. She had expected those feelings from her Father, but not from her Mother. She sighed, this reconciliation will take some doing; but I'm not running away again.

Chapter 7

The tearoom decorations were in keeping with the décor of the mall. Ivy vines climbing the wall with live plants in pots all over the room. It smelled heavenly, with the smell of fresh baked cinnamon rolls making her mouth water. There was only one person who could make smells that delicious and it had to be Lana, their next-door neighbor in her childhood home. The tables, covered with linen cloths each featured a flower in a vase. Lana had placed elegant antique cups and saucers in various curio cabinets and shelves scattered throughout the room. Lana, hurried in from the kitchen, "I thought I heard your voice Barb…oh my, Mara is that you?"

"Yes it's me, is that wonderful smell coming from your kitchen some of your homemade cinnamon rolls?"

"You'd better believe it. I must have had a sense you were coming. I remember when you were about six I would find you sitting on my back step just waiting for those rolls to come out of the oven." She winked at Mara; this was something she was sure Barbara hadn't known about. She knew how it had been over there, and so she gave Mara a little extra love and attention.

Mara reached out and gave Lana a big hug. "I remember those mornings Lana; they were always fresh and warm, and ready just before I left for school. Do you still have that wonderful icing that you put on them and are you still decorating those luscious cakes?"

"The answer is yes to all those questions. Only now, I have people that come from miles around here to sample my cinnamon rolls and order my cakes. I was able to retire early from my 8-5 job and started this little venture when my company offered early retirement to some of their employees three years ago. Now, let me pour you a cup of coffee, I have various flavors, my most popular is French Vanilla, then I will bring out those rolls you smelled." Then she was gone.

"Lana is still a whirlwind I can see, I am so happy she is living her dream"

"I will tell you Lana's story another time, she still lives next door and you might want to visit her and let her catch you up on what is happening in her life."

There was an awkward silence at the table, now that they were here sitting face-to-face neither one knew where to begin. Mara studied her Mother's face, she was showing her age, and there were lines around her eyes and frown lines etched in her cheeks. It must have been a rough eight years for her, she felt sorry that she had added to whatever her Mother had gone through. Yet, she was still certain in her heart that she had made the only choice she had then.

"Mother, how are you? How is Father? Are you both well? I see you are still working so your health must be good. You look like you are still doing quite a business and have even added a tanning bed. What did Father have to say about that?"

Barbara stared at her daughter and her face turned pale. "Your Father hasn't been to the shop in the last three years so he doesn't know, nor is he in a position to care. Mara, he had a heart attack and then a stroke after that about four years ago. He is in a wheelchair and rarely leaves the house. He's nearly helpless; the stroke left his right side paralyzed and useless. You know I've always catered to him. Now I am spending more time here. He's always frustrated and angry. I have a state worker that comes in every day to take care of his needs and a nurse that visits twice a week."

Mara trembled, that picture of her Father didn't match up to the strong, stern silent man of her childhood that would issue commands to both Mother and Daughter and expect instant responses.

"Can he speak? Does his mind still work? I am so sorry Mom." Mara felt the sting of tears in her eyes again. This looked like it would be a long day and here she was tearing up already. So much had changed and yet there was still a tension between them, words unsaid, looks that were unfathomable and uneasiness in her Mother's attitude.

"He understands everything that goes on around him. That's part of the problem; he sees situations he still wants to control and is unable to. He's frustrated, he slurs his words, and he's hard to understand. Occasionally he has a spell where his words come out the way they should, but not often. He just sits watching the Christian TV channel all-day, mouthing the words to the songs and the Bible verses. Sometimes, he just rocks and moans. I don't know what is going through his head. He can't explain, but all I see is rage and bitterness when he looks at me." Barbara covered her face for a moment, and then went on. "I think I know what he is agonizing over but I can't talk to him about it, it's just been too long and I want the past to stay in the past."

"That isn't possible now for me Mother. I came home to get some answers and they all deal with my past, your past and maybe events that happened before my birth. I don't know, I just know I had to come back to reconcile myself with my past before I could start to make a future for me."

"Mara, please don't open a can of worms. Spare you're Father and I that much. Please." Tears began streaming down her Mother's face. "Our home is so peaceful, do you have to come and change all that? There's no telling how he will react when he finds out you're here. As you can guess, he wasn't sorry to see you go. I had to grieve for you alone and in secret. You just don't understand."

"No Mother I don't understand, but I will understand before I leave this town again."

They drank their coffee in silence, Mara leaving her fresh cinnamon roll untouched as the words that she wanted to say, she held back. She didn't know how to make her Mother understand why she had to know about her life, her grandparents and why she was raised the way that she was. It would take a while. I might as well prepare myself for a long stay; start looking for a job and a place to live. Mara thought. It's going to be a long hard row to hoe, surprising herself by dredging that phrase up from her childhood.

"Oh there is my next customer, I need to go," said Barbara standing.

"Go ahead Mom; I will take care of the check. I want to visit with Lana anyway."

Chapter 8

The door chimed as her Mother went out, and Lana hurried out of the kitchen. "I didn't want to interrupt your conversation, but child, you haven't touched that roll, don't tell me I've lost my touch."

Mara smiled, "No, you haven't and I'm just preparing for the delightful taste in my mouth that I can still remember after all this time. No one in the world makes cinnamon rolls as well as you do. Do you have time to sit and talk for a while?"

"Sure, I don't have a large lunch crowd since the plant closed down, and those that do come in only ask for deli sandwiches and chips. Let's have a long talk."

Mara began to relax while Lana got up to refresh their coffee cups. Her Father insisted she not bother the neighbors, but there had been times that Lana had been the only source of comfort and happiness in her life. She remembered Lana and her husband with affection and always looked on with jealousy as their three children laughed and played in the backyard.

"How are your boys and Kristi doing? Do you have any grandchildren? I'm so happy to see you here and know you're doing what you've always wanted to do. This place is wonderful. Mmmmmm and these cinnamon rolls are even better than I remembered.

They taste like bread from heaven."

Lana began telling her about the years Mara had been away and her life in general now. Mara found that she was grandmother to two little grandsons and they were the light of her life. She pointed out their pictures on the wall behind Mara and beamed with pride when Mara told her how cute they were.

"Bob stays home now, he fell at the plant and is on disability, so he spends time with the grandsons, does yard work, and most of the housework. That leaves me the time to enjoy my Tearoom and my grandchildren. We're both well, even though Bob will always have a limp and he sometimes gets grumpy because he isn't working. Still, we're happy and we try to help your Mother with John as much as we can. Bob goes over each day just to sit with him for a while. We don't know if he wants Bob to be there, but he seems less agitated after he goes home."

"It must have been a rough four years for Mother."

"Yes, but she's come through it and is a stronger woman because of it. She's self-assured and able to break out of the mold your Father put her in while he was well and healthy. She updated her clothing, changed her hairstyle, and updated her cutting techniques by attending classes. She cuts almost everyone's hair in this town and the surrounding area. She added the tanning bed and someone is over there all the time. It only takes a few minutes to clean the bed after each customer and she does a load of towels every night anyway. I'm proud of her; she's come a long way. She felt guilty after you left. Your leaving didn't surprise anyone, least of all your Mom. They only marveled that you were able to stick it out till graduation."

"My Father? Did he even care?" Asked Mara.

"I'm sorry Mara; your leaving didn't bother him in the least. He even acted happy about it. Bob just couldn't understand why John would feel that way about his own daughter. After your Father had his stroke, he tried to talk to John about you, he became so agitated that we were afraid he'd have another stroke and not make it this time. We never mentioned your name again, and I'm sure your Mother didn't either."

Sorrowed but not surprised, Mara just nodded. She had known from early childhood that her Father would have been happier with just her Mother. She just didn't know or understand why. She was born when her parents were in their early 40's, not too old to have a child and financially they could afford to clothe and feed a baby.

"Well, I came back to see if I could get some of my own questions answered. I think it'll be hard to get them from Mother and it seems Father is unable to express his feelings to me now either." Sighing Mara took another sip of her coffee and ran her fingers through her hair. "I'll take it slow and easy for now. I'll be getting a job in Springfield or Decatur and stay here with Heather and Joe Davis until I find a job. I'll rent an apartment wherever my job takes me. It depends on how much I feel I need to be in contact with my parents to get my questions answered. Did you know my parents when they were expecting me?"

"I'm sorry honey, we moved next door when you were almost a year old. In fact, I made your first birthday cake. Your father didn't want to celebrate in any way and I couldn't just let the day slide by; you were a wonderful, adorable baby! You never cried and were always quiet and smiling. Your eyes were the most amazing color of green, and I can see they haven't changed a bit. I always loved your eyes."

"That's one thing I've always wondered about. My eyes are a distinct color of green and my parents and everyone in their family have blue eyes. Don't you think that's a little strange?"

Looking away, Lana spoke softly, "It could have been a longtime ago that someone in their family had those green eyes. It could be a recessive gene."

Not convinced but Mara decided not to upset her friend any more by trying to explore the past. She wiped the icing from the corners of her mouth preparing to leave. "I'll see you soon Lana, I'll be around, I need to explore the town and think."

"Honey, there will be some who won't be happy you are back, but there will be those of us who loved and missed you. Hang on to that thought."

Mara gave Lana a hug and kiss on the cheek. Lana handed her a package of rolls to take home to Heather and Joe with her love. Joe often stopped in for coffee when he was working in this area and was obviously a favored customer.

"Bye Mara, be careful when you stir the pot that you don't burn yourself." With those words ringing in her ears, Mara left the tearoom, more puzzled then ever but more determined to find her past while she talked to those in the present.

Chapter 9

Mara stopped in the antique shop and said hello to Nancy, but cut their visit short, there was just too much that she had to do and find out.

It was a mild day for late October, the sun was shining brightly, and the air was warm enough to do without a jacket. She strolled up one side of Main Street and down the other, trying to remember what the storefronts used to be. Some she knew because they were here when she left, others she just knew by her parents stories. The movie house was of course gone; Bullitt was the last movie shown there, not a trace of it remained to say where it had been. She went over to the park and chose a bench where she could watch people as they walked by. She wasn't sure what direction to take next and she needed time to absorb all the events that happened today.

Why was there such a mystery now? Why didn't people want her to dig in her past? Why did her Mother say, "Don't open a can of worms"? Then there was the remark Lana had made about getting burned by stirring the pot. She just didn't know what to think and she didn't have a clue where to go next. She needed to clear her head. She decided to take a drive to the edge of town and visit Riverside cemetery. Visiting the cemetery and her grandparent's grave would be soothing. She also wanted to look for some of the old tombstones and markers she remembered as a child. She loved to explore old cemeteries; this one and Wilcox were her favorites when she was small. She would sometimes stop at one of them after school if she thought her Mom would still be at the shop and her Dad still working. She was the only person she knew that loved to visit old burial grounds. She visited some cemeteries in California while she was there. It was peaceful and always relaxed her to walk among the graves and try to imagine what secrets they held.

The Cavalier had a sunroof; she flipped it open and began to drive. The trees were still colorful but the leaves were falling fast and one good hard rain would bring them all down. She drove slowly through town, absorbing the sights and noting the differences. What was once a bowling alley was now the second tavern, so she was sure there wasn't much for kids to do here? Even less than when she was a teenager and that was saying something. She didn't do much her life had been so restricted. She had chores to do after school, and she was responsible for having dinner on the table when her parents came home from work. If dinner happened to be in a slow cooker in the morning, she knew she would have a little time to visit her favorite places.

She pulled in the drive of the cemetery and was a little dismayed. It wasn't as well-kept as it had been in the past. She cringed to see even her grandparents grave markers buried under pine needles and decayed leaves. She tenderly knelt to clean them off with a tissue she found in her purse. She remembered them but only vaguely. Killed in a car crash when Mara was four she remembered the scents she associated with them. Grandma smelled like vanilla and Grandpa always smelled like Old Spice.

The stone read:

Ellen and Calvin Bishop

In Love and Together Always

April 17, 1982

She said a silent prayer then stood up and walked around. She saw a couple of headstones for a couple of children she had baby-sat for when she was a teenager. She reminded herself to ask Heather what the circumstances were surrounding their passing.

It was nearly time for her to be back at Heather and Joe's and she still wanted to go to Johnson's Market to pick up a Decatur and Springfield paper. She might as well start looking for a job. She couldn't stay with her best friend forever and she'd feel better if she had the freedom to come and go as she pleased without worrying about disturbing their family.

Johnson's wasn't busy so she took her time, looking to see if she could find some snacks to take home to the little ones. After she picked up her papers, she found a bag of Smarties and remembering how much the children she baby-sat for loved them, she decided they were just the snack to take home to JJ and Melody. Even Melody could have them if watched. Grabbing a diet Pepsi, she drove back to the comfortable house she called home right now.

Letting herself in with her key, she detected the aroma of pot roast simmering in the crock-pot.

Mmmm, smelled delicious and made her realize she hadn't stopped to have lunch. Snagging an apple from the fruit basket, she decided it would hold her until dinner. It was her favorite snack, apple, and diet Pepsi.

Spreading the papers out on the table, she read the classified ads while she munched on her apple. There were a few possibilities; she could ask Joe if she could use his computer to update her resume, or she could use her laptop. She also made plans to go to Springfield to take the state test at the beginning of the week. Sunday papers would have the biggest job selection and she didn't have to be in a big hurry. She might as well take her time and find a job she would enjoy. Finding a place to live would be a little harder. It would depend on where a job was found. She could stay in either Decatur or Springfield, or even stay in Illiopolis since it was about halfway between the two cities. Those decisions could wait until later; right now, she was overwhelmed with trying to understand everything she'd heard since coming home. In addition, the emotional impact of being back in the same place she had run away from those long years ago left her feeling drained.

Chapter 10

She was still reading the papers when she heard Heather and her kids' come in the front door. Heather came in with a sleeping Melody in her arms and JJ trailing behind with a handful of papers.

"Look, see what I did at school today." His smile was so big and it showed off his dimples. "It's a pumpkin 'cause it's almost Halloween. Know what I'm going to be? Spiderman. I love Spiderman don't you?" He got his Mom's chattering gene, Mara thought.

"Sure I do." Mara replied. "Do you have the movie? If not, we'll rent it at the video store and watch it this weekend."

"Yes we have the movie, can we have popcorn too?"

"Sure." Answered his Mom, "and for a special treat a glass of root beer. Now up to your room and change into play clothes, its warm enough today you can play outside till Daddy gets home if he isn't too late."

JJ scampered up the stairs and they could hear his feet pounding down the hall to his bedroom. They laughed at his high spirits. Mara gave Heather a quick rundown of what she'd accomplished that day, including looking in the papers for a job and a place to live.

"Mom, I'm going out to ride my scooter for a while, don't worry I have a jacket on and my old shoes on. Love you," JJ said as he went out the front door.

Heather bustled around the kitchen preparing gravy for the roast and potatoes that had been simmering all-day, setting the table and throwing a tossed salad together.

"Joe will be home around six this evening. An early night for a change, so we can sit and talk. Maybe we'll watch a movie with JJ and let him have his popcorn and root beer."

Mara marveled at the ordinary events they were talking about doing. Watching a movie and having a special night with her son, Daddy would be there with them. It was not something she experienced at her home. How awesome to have a relationship like that. The more she was around this family, the happier she became. Their happiness radiated around them.

Her friend picked up her cell phone to call her husband, and Mara set the table for their meal. Remembering where the glasses were, she took some down and put ice in them for their drinks, and the kid's juice. It felt good to be useful and to feel surrounded by a loving atmosphere. I could live like this, she thought.

The dinner hour passed swiftly after Joe came home. Melody again entertained them with her antics trying to learn to feed herself. Heather stayed calm, not worrying about the floor or her daughter's hair.

The evening went by fast and she was sorry to have it end, but JJ was nearly asleep on the sofa, and Melody had fallen asleep on the floor with her blanket in her hand.

Mara said, "You know, it's been a long day, and I think I'll leave you two alone and go to my room. Thanks so much for welcoming me into your home." She gave Heather a hug and a kiss on the cheek and went to bed. She needed her rest, next week was going to be a big week of job-hunting, and she wanted to feel refreshed, she intended to take it easy this weekend.

Chapter 11

The weekend passed like a whirlwind and soon it was the beginning of the workweek. Joe was working and Heather planned to take JJ to school and run some errands. Mara drove over to Johnson's Market and bought both a Springfield and a Decatur paper again. She planned to go to Springfield today to take the test to qualify her for a state job. She knew the job part would not be easy, finding one would take some time. They were downsizing under budget constraints but she would try that route anyway. She looked at the Decatur paper, not much there but she had a little time before she would start running out of money.

She was upset she didn't hear from her Mother this past weekend, even though she had given her a cell phone number to call. She explained she'd always have that with her, and always turned on; she could always leave a voicemail message. She wondered if her Father knew of her homecoming yet, and if so, what was his reaction. She knew she would have to bide her time and be patient. Barbara and John didn't do anything without first looking at the situation from all angles. She could wait, she'd waited this long.

She opened her closet door and inspected her wardrobe. She chose a smooth black skirt with a scalloped edge with turtle neck and flowing poncho to round out her wardrobe.

Heels were necessary to go looking for work, so she took out her most comfortable pair of dress shoes and put them on.

Mara took her laptop computer down from the shelf. Joe's modem was set up for wireless access, which was another tool to help her find a job. Her resumes were printed on good professional paper also a list of her references. She could print her cover letters on Joe's printer. Checking to make sure she had her cell phone in her purse, she went out to the car. She was ready for the challenge. Being in temp service in San Francisco made her confident she could find a job that would be rewarding and challenging. She learned early in her career that she was a people person and most of her shyness disappeared since her confidence level went up.

She tuned in to one of the local country stations and started toward Springfield. She sang with the radio when one of her favorite tunes came on and watched the landscape as she went by. Not much to see, she recognized the mounded bunkers where the ammunition plant had been during the war. She thought, if those walls could talk, what stories they would tell. In fact, this area of the state was rich in history. Springfield and Decatur both had many historic sites because Abraham Lincoln had lived in this area. She would make one of her top priorities to see the new Lincoln Library in Springfield, and she longed to see New Salem State Park. She loved the atmosphere and the drama of it all. She was a history buff, and she was excited to be back in her home state to see all the sites she hadn't seen as a child. That one school trip to New Salem had fired her imagination and given her a love of history.

Mara was in Springfield in fewer than 30 minutes. She found her way off the interstate and to the Stratton building located in the Capitol complex. She knew she could take the test here for state employment on Mondays, Wednesdays, and Fridays. This is where her job search would begin. Finding a parking place wasn't easy on a busy Monday morning in the Capitol Area but she found a spot about two blocks from the building.

The air was crisp but sunny, she was glad she remembered to pack her warmest jacket before she left the Bay area. She would need it in the coming months. I do need to shop for a winter coat, she thought.

As she expected, the test wasn't hard and she knew she passed with flying colors. She put down her county preferences as Sangamon and Macon counties then left the building. Back in the bright sunlight again, she began walking. She wanted to acquaint herself with the downtown area. She hadn't had any reason to be in Springfield before she left home so she wanted to look around, pick up a rental-housing guide and check out the area. Walking for a while she found herself in the historic district, open to foot traffic and lost herself in the restored homes and museums. She stared in awe at the home of Abraham and Mary Todd Lincoln. This is a home she wanted to see. She paid her small admission fee and took the tour of the house; it was beautiful, but homey at the same time. Just the house she would imagine the 16th president would live in. When finished, she moved on to the other historic sites and toured a few, or stopped in the front to admire the architecture of the period. She would explore this area when she had more time. Maybe Heather would like to come over with her one-day, have a ladies day out. That sounded like fun and she was hungry for fun right now. She had lived such a lonely life in San Francisco, with no close friends or family around. It felt nice to be part of a loving family like Joe and Heather's. She sighed, walking the few blocks back to her car. She needed to drive back to Illiopolis, she wanted to fix dinner tonight for them, but could only do that if she got home before they did.

Chapter 12

Pulling into the driveway, she found she was already the last one home. Walking into the house, she could hear the kids playing in the dining room, the TV was on in the living room, and Joe was sitting in his favorite chair. Delicious smells were drifting toward her from the kitchen.

"Hi Mara," said Joe. "Heather is in the kitchen trying out a new recipe. I'm just resting for a bit, I need to go back to work to cover for a guy who's sick."

Mara stopped in the dining room and got down on the floor with the kids, they were playing with building blocks. JJ was stacking them and Melody was busy knocking them down. There were hoots of laughter coming from each child. Smiling she went on to the kitchen.

"What's that delicious smell?"

"I have a divine recipe from one of the Mother's at PTA and decided to try it tonight. We're also having some fresh baked bread, straight from Lana's shop. Are you hungry, did you find anything interesting? Do you have any leads? Was the test for the state jobs hard?"

"Hey slow down. I didn't find out much today. I took the state test in Springfield and then wandered around looking at the sites. Not too productive huh? Still, I feel relaxed, refreshed, and confident. If I don't find anything in Springfield, then I will head to Decatur."

"Mara, could you set the table for me? This stir-fry chicken will be ready in just a few moments."

"Sure," she said as she headed toward the cabinets. "I will clean the kitchen tonight so you can have some time with Joe before he heads back to work. I'll even bathe the kids for you and all you will need to do is tuck them in."

"Now that's an offer I can't refuse."

Dinnertime passed as pleasantly as it always did. Mara enjoyed talking, laughing, and watching the kids. They were so sweet, but of course, she had always loved children and she already loved these two little ones. JJ had started calling her Aunt Mara; Melody couldn't say that too well so she was Mar-Mar to her. She had to be careful, she was getting comfortable here, and it would only be a matter of time before she'd need to find her own place. She decided she wouldn't live here in Illiopolis. Whether she found a job in Springfield or Decatur she was still close enough to her parents and the family she had grown to love. She felt that she needed to be close to both of them. Tomorrow she would go back to her Mother's shop and try to get closer to her. She wanted to know if her Father knew she was back. There were so many things she wanted to know. Questions, questions running through her head, would they ever be answered?

Joe was preparing to leave for his extra time on patrol, Heather was kissing him good-bye at the door, and the children were sitting on the stairs waiting for their Mommy to tuck them into bed.

"Good-bye Joe, be careful and know we love you and pray for you while you are gone."

"Night JJ, night Melody. Daddy will see you tomorrow. Sleep tight. I love you two and you too." He said as he kissed Heather again. Then he was gone.

Mara went to the living room and waited for Heather to finish the children's bedtime routine. Joe had built a fire in the fireplace and brought in a couple of extra logs so it would be cozy tonight. Heather breezed into the room. "I'm sorry; the kids just had to have one more story tonight."

"Not a problem," Mara replied. "I was just thinking of how to approach my Mom again. She got so upset last week when I was trying to talk to her. I felt she wanted to see me again, but she was so worried about what Father would say."

"What are your plans for tomorrow Mara? I help in JJ's class on Tuesdays, and Melody will be with my Mom. Joe said to tell you to go ahead and use his computer if you want to, especially if you need something printed. Everything you would need is in plain sight in his office."

"You two have been so great to me. I don't know how I'll ever repay you for what you're doing for me."

"Mara, I always felt guilty after you left, I felt I had failed you as a friend. I wanted so much to help you, but I didn't know how. I didn't know what you were going through and I probably still don't, but do know this. I am your friend and I will always be here for you. You are welcome to stay with us as long as you need to."

Mara's eyes were stinging with unshed tears. She was beginning to understand what true friendship meant, and it was comforting being a part of this wonderful family.

She replied, "I intend to go to see Mother again tomorrow and maybe talk again to Lana, and I want to visit with Nancy as well. Someone has to remember when I was born. What were my parents like before? Why did they change so much after Mother became pregnant? So many questions, I have to know some answers, I just have to!"

"You will Mara, I know you will and I'll help you all I can, and so will Joe."

"Thanks you always were and always will be my one true friend. I could always count on you, and you didn't fail me in anyway. In fact, if it weren't for your party, I wouldn't have had the window of opportunity to leave when I did."

"What did you do when you left? Tell me a little more of the past eight years."

"There isn't much to tell, I enrolled myself in night classes and worked in a restaurant during the day. I found public relations were my strong point so I worked toward getting a degree in that field. Meanwhile, I moved up in the restaurant until I was head hostess and was helping the owner promote business. Practicing what I was learning in my classes. He was grateful to me, and when I left, he gave me a good severance package and told me I could always have a free meal at Papa Leo's."

"You seem so different now, confident and happy with your life. How did that happen?"

"I got involved in a group therapy and then private counseling for a while. All along, I knew I would eventually need to come home and face my past. You're right, I'm different, and I'm able to hold my head up and be proud of whom I am. I'm not perfect but I've accepted that and it's been the turning point in my life."

"Well, I like the new and improved version, even more then when you were 18. Now, let's pop some popcorn and watch a good movie and have a good cry so we can start fresh tomorrow."

They enjoyed the rest of the evening, sharing small talk and a few tears while watching a movie then saying goodnight they went to bed.

Chapter 13

The next morning, Mara dressed in jeans and a sweatshirt hustled down to the tearoom. Her mother always had a cup of coffee before her customers came in and she wanted a chance to talk to her.

"Good morning Lana."

"Mara nice to see you again, your Mother should be here any minute."

"I know, she always comes in to get a cup of coffee and a little chat before her first customers come, that's why I'm here. This morning the chat will be with me."

Lana went back to the kitchen to get Mara a cup of coffee and a fresh baked roll. Meanwhile Mara fidgeted. How was she going to start this conversation? What should she say? She guessed that it would follow its own course. She knew patience wasn't one of her strong points but she was anxious to find out all she could from her Mother.

The bell over the door jangled and Barbara walked in, taken aback to see Mara sitting in the corner table.

"Goodness Mara, what brings you out so early?" She said as she took her jacket off.

"I wanted to talk to you and find out how Father is doing. I'd like to see him."

"Well, I haven't told him you were back yet. He didn't have a good weekend and I didn't want to upset him more."

"Mother, this is Tuesday; I will see him by Friday. You'll need to tell him or I'll show up on your doorstep. Nothing you can do or say that will keep me from seeing him. You know I adore him, even though he acted as if I didn't exist."

"All right, I'll tell him between now and Friday, and since you are insisting, you might as well come for dinner. I'll schedule myself light that afternoon and will have something in the crock pot."

"Great. I have some news that I would prefer to tell you both at the same time. I need to know a little family history and I think you can help me with that."

The blood drained from Barbara's face as she stared openmouthed at her daughter. "You want to know family history? Why? Both sets of grandparents are dead and your Father and I didn't have any brothers or sisters. That's all there is to know."

With that, Barbara stood up and stalked out the door.

"Whew, she didn't even wait for her coffee. I think I'll run it over to her so she'll have it. I hope everything is all right. I thought it would be good for you to come home, especially with the way that John is right now." She was still muttering as she walked quickly next door to the salon. Well that was tactful. Mara thought. She picked up the Decatur paper that someone had left on the next table. Flipping through the classified ads, she stopped. Here's one worth exploring, Mara thought.

Millikin University. Do you have experience in Public Relations? Do you love working with people? We have an immediate opening for an Activity Coordinator to work between the admissions office and the Alumni Association. You'll be promoting activities, writing press releases and be the liaison between students, faculty, and alumni. Please bring a resume and references to the main office. Salary and benefits negotiable, Millikin University is an Equal Opportunity Employer.

That sounds like it is a job made for me. I know exactly where it is, and it is something I would enjoy. She left money for her breakfast on the table and was ready to leave when Lana came back from delivering the coffee.

"Bye Lana, got a good lead on a job, I need to hustle home to change clothes so I can drive to Decatur. Wish me luck."

Chapter 14

She drove to Heather and Joe's house; all was quiet as usual at this time of day. Going to her room, she selected an outfit from her closet that would be suitable for an interview. The job sounded too good to be true and she knew it would be something she'd love doing.

Driving east to Decatur, she was optimistic, singing with the radio, happy for the moment. The bright sunshine melted away her worries and fears. It was a perfect autumn day and she was excited by the possibilities. She had taken the time to explore the school's website and surfed for more information about Decatur. It looked like a good place to live and to work.

She followed the Millikin University signs off the interstate, turning down West Main and driving toward the university, she marveled at the trees that lined the street and the beautiful colors at this time of year. Nice homes here as well, and if she decided to move to Decatur, she knew there were plenty of apartments around. In fact, there was one right on that corner for rent, only about six blocks from the University. She would wait to see how the interview went and come back to write down the phone number from the sign.

Following the signs to the administration building, she parked. What a beautiful campus, I would feel comfortable working here. Pull yourself together girl and make a good first impression. She had begun her positive talk while she was seeing a therapist in San Francisco, just trying to deal with a disease that would eventually cause blindness. She learned from those sessions and used what she learned nearly every day. Taking a couple of deep cleansing breaths, she got out of her car.

Sycamore leaves crunched under her heels as she walked to the main office building. She carried her portfolio with her resume and references at her side. She knew she looked professional and felt a sense of calmness as she walked to her destination.

A young woman greeted her as she walked into the office. "Good morning. May I help you?"

Mara replied, "I'm here to apply for the job that's in the paper."

"Sure, and the woman that is doing the interviewing is in right now. Let me take your resume to her."

Mara took a seat and looked around at her surroundings. The office was neat and cheerful with plants and personal photographs on the two desks that made up the reception area. The receptionist came with another woman following her. The young woman went back to her desk, her desk plate said her name was Beth, and the older woman came around the counter holding out her hand.

"Hello, I am Carol Matthews, Dean Hall's assistant. He's in a meeting right now and asked that I give you an initial interview. I looked over your resume and you're the most qualified person we've had so far. Come on back to my office."

Mara eagerly followed Carol back to her office. She passed small offices along the hallway, most occupied busy. Everyone stopped what he or she were doing and gave a smile or small wave while going by. They entered Carol's office. Tastefully decorated, she had various pictures of the many buildings that made up the university, including the new science building. She's a proud grandmother of two grandchildren, looking at the pictures lined up on the window ledge. I'm impressed, thought Mara.

"Mara, tell me a little bit about yourself. Why do you think you could fill this position? I've read your resume and will be contacting your references, but I want you to tell me what your strong points are."

Mara smiled she knew she liked Carol already.

"I enjoy working with people, I'm organized and love working in Public Relations. I get along with both the older generation as well as the younger. I'm detail oriented and have worked with the public in many different situations. I believe I would be an asset to this office and to the university."

Carol, looking over Mara's resume said, "You have all the qualifications we are looking for, but tell me, what brings you back to the Midwest?"

"I have elderly parents and wanted to spend some time with them while I still can. They couldn't come to me, so I came home to them. Right now, I'm staying with my best friend in Illiopolis. Her family has allowed me to stay in their guest room until I get my bearings."

"Will you be living in Decatur if you find work here?" Carol asked.

"Yes, in fact, I passed a nice apartment building with a For Rent sign in the front as I was driving to the University."

Carol sat drumming her fingers and looking over Mara's references and resume. "So far, we haven't had anyone as qualified as you applying for this job. Are you prepared to start work at the beginning of next week? If so, I'll give my recommendation to the Dean, and we'll give you a call by Thursday."

"Great," said Mara already feeling good about her chances.

"Oh we do have some nice perks that go with the job," Carol continued. "If you would like to take a class or two, you can do so tuition free, if you can work around your work schedule. Hours will be flexible, sometimes busier then others. You will be busiest during Freshman Arrival Week, Parents Weekend and of course Homecoming. You also have free access to the fitness center that's just a block away from the main campus." She stood up and held out her hand. "I'm confident that you'll fit in well with the rest of the staff."

Dazed at how fast things were moving, she shook hands with Carol and walked back down the hall to the reception area. Beth looked up from her desk, smiling and gave Mara a little wink. "Hope to see you again real soon."

Mara almost skipped down the sidewalk, she was confidant that she would be getting this position and was elated. Now if everything else fell into place she would be happy with her life again. She knew she was capable of doing the work, and she felt comfortable in the environment and the people she'd met were friendly. She felt it was a good work atmosphere and she hoped she received the offer. She didn't ask about salary, there was enough time for that later and she valued a good work environment over high pay anyway. The cost of living here would be much less then in San Francisco and she wouldn't have to use up her savings account if she found a job right away.

This was going better then expected. She drove around the neighborhood to get familiar with the area. She found all the usual fast-food spots she liked, a grocery store in a small strip mall that included a tanning place, nail salon and even a Dollar General store. She could see living in this area. She also had noticed a park that looked inviting with a bike and walking trail. Yes, this will be an excellent neighborhood to live in.

She dialed Heather from her cell phone. "Heather, guess what? I may have a job. Let's celebrate, I will bring home Chinese take out for dinner tonight. I talked to my Mother this morning and I can't wait to get your feelings on everything that is happening."

Chapter 15

After dinner, the dishes cleared away, and the children put to bed, Joe, Heather, and Mara sat down to talk about her day. She was happy for the feedback she got from Joe about the area where she had seen the apartment and the general area of the university.

"If I am thinking of the right place, I believe there is a city police officer that lives in another building in that block and that particular apartment has underground parking. You'd be secure there. Sounds like a great opportunity for you but don't feel like you have to move out as soon as you find a job."

"Oh, I don't, but I feel like I am imposing on your family and I'm used to being independent. I've been on my own for the last eight years."

Joe was funny and a little silly from being so tired. He started telling stories about funny things he'd seen on the job. Mara mentioning seeing deer on the drive over from Springfield brought out a funny story.

"That reminds me of a time when I received a call to stand by a man who'd hit two deer. When I arrived at the site one of them had limped off the road back into the woods. The other one wasn't dead yet, but you could tell he wasn't going to make it. I hated to see it hurting, but I had to wait for the department of Conservation people to get there. They would have to be the one to put him out of his misery. This beat-up, rusted old pickup pulled up and a shirtless man in bib overalls jumped out of it. His two daughters also climbed out of the truck. They were clapping their hands saying 'Daddy's gonna get us a deer, a deer for us.' Dancing around in the snow slush, one of them was even barefoot. The guy walked over and asked if he could have the deer and he pulled out a big ole knife preparing to finish the deer off. I told him; no, he couldn't do anything until the Conservation men came. They would have the say if he could take the deer or not. The buck was still thrashing, the young women were still dancing and clapping, and the man looked like he couldn't wait to sink that knife into that deer's throat. Finally, the Conservation people got there. They looked at the deer, decided it wouldn't live and told the man he could have it. Those girls were so excited. The man reached in the truck and brought out an old coat that he put over the poor deer's head before he cut its throat." That was the weirdest experience I have ever had. He loaded the deer into the back of his old pick up truck and off they went."

The girls laughed at the story and marveled at people, but then who knows; maybe the deer would feed his family for part of the winter. Mara was glad that a family would have something to eat for the winter. She knew from when she was in school and before she got her first part-time job, what it was like to not know for sure where her next meal was coming from.

Joe tired from working the double shift the night before, said his good nights and went to bed. "Good luck with the job." He called from the foot of the stairs.

They sat quietly for a few minutes, basking in the warmth of the fire and in their friendship. With a friendship like theirs, no words needed to be spoken. It was comfortable to be lost in their own thoughts for a while.

"Heather, I…"

"Mara, what…"

Laughing Mara said, "Just like it used to be with both of us wanting to talk at the same time. You're the only one I felt I could talk to."

"Well, go ahead and tell me how it went with your Mom today."

"Oh, the bad start of the day. She hasn't told Father yet that I'm home, and she looks as if she's scared of talking about the past. I don't understand what's happening; I just want to know the health history of my family."

"It does seem a little strange her acting like that. My Mom told me they kept your birth quiet. They didn't make a big announcement and you'd think someone who was finally having a baby late in life would be happy about it and show her off to the world. She said she didn't even bring you to Church for several months. Everyone thought you were sick, but when they started taking you places, Mom said you looked healthy."

Mara answered, "Do you know there are few pictures of me as a child or a teenager for that matter?"

"Well you might learn something new when you go over on Friday for dinner. She'll have told your Father you're back and maybe he's softened his attitude since he had his stroke."

"I'm not counting on it. I do want to see him though."

"Sure that's normal, it isn't normal the way your Mom is reacting to you being home after not seeing you for eight years."

Changing the subject Heather asked, "What are you going to do for the next couple of days while you wait for your phone call from Millikin?"

Mara smiled, "I'm going to go look at that apartment on West Main that has the for rent sign on it, I'm so sure that I'll get this job."

"You'll need furniture and that means…"

"Shopping" they said at the same time. Laughing they decided on that note that it was time to go to bed.

Mara laid awake thinking of what she would need to start up a new apartment. Mentally she started making a list of items to buy. She'd given her household supplies to a young neighbor with a small child before she left San Francisco. She was still making her list when she fell asleep.

She was walking in a long hallway; she could hear a woman crying but couldn't tell from which room the cries were coming. She opened each door as she came to it; the hallway seemed to go on forever. The cries were getting louder, she thought she was getting closer, a new cry was heard, that of a newborn baby. She could hear a man's voice and he was screaming. What was he saying? She edged closer so she could hear, but just when she was beginning to hear the words, she saw a door swing open and the man hurrying out. She couldn't tell who it was, but could tell by the way he was stalking down the hall he wasn't happy. Still she heard the cries of the woman and the cries of the baby. She went to the door still slightly open. Pushing the door opened wider she looked in. There was the woman, she was holding a baby, and by the color of the blanket, it must be a girl. The woman's face, hidden in the folds of the blanket was sobbing her heart out. "How could he go behind my back and name you Mara! He knew I wanted to call you Catherine." The woman looked up, it was her own Mother. The baby must be her.

The jangling alarm yanked the dream from her as she awoke to the present. Now what was that about, she thought? It made her uneasy and she tried to remember all the parts of her dream. It'd been so real. Did it have something to do with her birth? Well, she'd know soon enough. She hoped to know more after dinner with her parents on Friday night.

Chapter 16

Wednesday promised to be a typical central Illinois fall day; dreary, overcast skies and a slight drizzle of rain. Mara showered and put on a pair of jeans and a shirt. Pulling her hair back in a barrette she put on her usual small amount of make up and was ready for her day.

Mara woke to find Heather puttering around in the kitchen, she handed her a cup of coffee as she walked in the door.

"Good morning, I am playing hooky today from everything and going with you to look at that apartment and go shopping." Heather laughed, "I didn't ask, but I thought you probably wouldn't mind. I know where to go in Decatur to get some good deals and some fun places for accessories. Can I go? Please?" She giggled. To Mara, it was just like Junior High again. Heather, my best friend, always the one with the ready laugh and the fun loving nature and always ready to help someone at the drop of a hat.

Mara walked over and gave her a hug. It felt awkward at first; she hadn't been raised to be a hugging, touching person. Heather hugged her back, with tears in her eyes and said, "I'm so happy you are back, you're so much more relaxed and open."

"Well I've gained a new understanding of myself in my therapy, and that is one thing I'm learning to do. Allowing myself to be open to people is scary, but I'm determined to have a different life than my parents. I learned my childhood was not normal and now I'm searching for my true self. I know it's in here somewhere."

"Well, ok then, let's get ourselves ready to go. I have all day and Joe will be home when JJ gets out of school and Mom has Melody for the day. Don't worry; she would take her every day if I'd let her. Mom's also making us a casserole so all we have to do when we get home is pop it in the oven."

"Great." Said Mara. "I have my cell phone, in case the University wants to call me today instead of tomorrow. I need some of your good taste to help me furnish an apartment in low-budget chic."

They decided to take Heather's minivan in case they found big items they would need to transport home. Her seats folded down with no problem and she pulled out both car seats so they would have plenty of room. The drive to Decatur was hilarious, Heather excited and looking forward to spending the day with her best friend and Mara caught up in the happiness of the moment. Worries about her illness, the meeting with her parents, nothing was going to spoil the day for her.

"The apartment is right on the corner of West Main and South Dennis. You can't miss it going east on Main."

"Ok, we'll take down the phone number and make the call while we're enjoying some breakfast at Panera's. They have the best bagels in the area, and I have been craving a cinnamon bagel, what do you say?"

"It sounds good to me. I'm so glad you wanted to come with me today, the rain was getting me down a little and I was starting to stew about Friday night and even worry maybe I wouldn't get the job at the University." Mara shook her head, "I've come a long way, but still have doubts about my own abilities sometimes. Once an ugly duckling, always an ugly duckling, but I'm still trying to turn into a swan."

Heather laughed, "Mara, you are not an ugly duckling, you need to take a good hard look in your mirror and see the real you. I love your down to earth attitude and your willingness to be open to other people. It has to be hard overcoming the kind of childhood you lived. I'm proud of you."

Turning a bright red, Mara could only stare at her friend. She hadn't realized that Heather knew her so well. It was great to know she had someone she could talk to and depend on. She hadn't seen anyone else from High School yet; she didn't know how she would react to those that had been mean to her. She knew she had always been the brunt of many jokes and caught many behind the hand whispers as she passed groups in the hall. Her Mother was the only beauty operator in town, but still Mara's hair was out of date. Her Mother just didn't care or her Father wouldn't let her care. She didn't know which.

"There's the building, and the sign is still there. Turn down Dennis street and let me look at it from all angles," Mara suggested. "I need to write down the phone number as well.

They parked the van and walked around the building. It seemed nice, brick, landscaped yard, and Joe was right, an underground garage opened by a remote control. The houses around were well-kept; single-family homes on Dennis looked lovingly cared for.

"Look Heather, this street is actually brick. How cool is that?"

"Let's go for breakfast and call that number, I can't wait to see the inside."

"I'll call her on the way, maybe we can set up an appointment to look at it and find out what the rent is," said Mara.

They drove down West Main, Mara pointed out the administration building where she hoped to be working soon. Lori was the name of the woman who answered the ringing phone. Mara introduced herself to Lori and inquired about the apartment on Main Street. After a short conversation, they made an appointment to see the apartment at 10a.m.that morning. That would give them time to have breakfast.

Mara allowed the excitement to take over, the rent was reasonable, much less than she expected and the lease terms were good. The deposit and first month's rent she would be able to make with no problem. She hoped it was as appealing on the inside as it looked from the outside.

"Look Mara, this is an easy straight path to get to most of the places you would need to find. On the North end of town, you'll find the mall, Wal-Mart and just about anywhere else you may want to shop."

"Look at the flowers," Mara exclaimed. "They're beautiful even now."

"Decatur has a Million Flower Project in the works, to brighten up the roads into town. They're working on renovating downtown area and there's some marvelous shopping on Merchant Street as well as a few good restaurants."

Heather continued, "Joe works over here quite a lot, he knows where all the good places are. He gets around being a State Trooper; he's looked into a few cases over here. They do have campus security in place. They found a coed murdered a few years ago, and they've never found her killer. They have security phones in place all over campus.

"Oh that's a comforting thought," laughed Mara. "I hope I hear from them soon, I am anxious to get back to work, doing what I'm good at."

Chapter 17

The small eatery was not busy so they sat and lingered over their coffee and chatted. Heather whispered, "Don't look now Mara, but the guy at the table across from us is checking you out."

"No way."

"Yes way," replied Heather just like kids again. "I think it's someone we went to high school with but I can't think of his name."

Peeking, Mara caught her breath, it was Jerry Lowe, and she had a crush on him in her freshman year. He stood up and walked over to their table.

"Heather, do you remember me? We went to school together in Illiopolis. I live and work in Decatur now, but wanted to stop and say hello."

"Hi Jerry, you remember Mara Conley don't you?"

Jerry did a double-take, "uhhh, of course, how are you Mara?"

Mara knew he didn't have a clue about who she was, but she fought back the impulse to pull into her protective shell. "Hi Jerry, nice to see you again." She held out her hand and he took it, holding it a tad longer than normal.

Jerry inquired, "Mara, are you living around here again? I remember you left town after graduation, didn't you?" He glanced at her left hand as she was checking out his. No wedding rings, she felt herself relax.

"I have a job opportunity at Millikin. I came back because my parents are elderly and I want to be close to them, in case they need me."

"I see, are they still in Illiopolis? I don't get over there much unless I'm shooting pool there with my pool team. We shoot at Habits and Vices a couple of times a session. All my family lives and work around Decatur now. The plant shutting down forced my Dad into early retirement and my sister already lived here, so they sold their home and moved to a retirement community on the South side of town."

"Yes, Mom still runs her beauty salon; Dad suffered a heart attack and stroke and doesn't leave the house." She looked at her watch, "I'm sorry, but we have an appointment in about 20 minutes and we need to leave."

Heather was behind him shaking her head giving her signs to keep on talking.

"No problem, I have an appointment myself then also. Do you have a phone number I can use to call you?"

Mara hesitated. Heather took over, "Here's my phone number, and she'll be with my husband and I for a while. Call her anytime. If no one answers, you can leave a message for her." She was smiling as she sized him up.

"All right, I will give you a ring, maybe we can have dinner together some time?"

All Mara could do was shake her head yes. Am I doomed to feel this way forever, like the person I was? I feel like a stuttering teenager being asked for her first date. Come on girl; pretend you are meeting him at a cable car stop in San Francisco.

"We need to get to our appointments," Jerry said. "I'll be calling you soon" and with a long last look, he left the restaurant.

"I think you made a conquest. I really do, now don't tell me that you aren't interested in having a man in your life, because I just won't believe it." Heather said.

For the second time that morning, Mara blushed. "I didn't have a good experience with the one man I had a relationship with and I gave up finding someone. I'm afraid to have a marriage like my Mother and Father's. Your marriage, though, seems so happy and, well…perfect."

Heather laughed aloud, "Perfect? No not perfect but we have a wonderful marriage; we love each other even with our defects and flaws. JJ and Melody have brought us closer together. I worry about him, about his safety, and he feels he leaves his family alone too much, but we deal with whatever comes. That's why we have Rascal and Culprit. No one comes on the property that we don't know."

Mara reflected on that last statement. Could marriage be that way? She hadn't known anything but tension and strife in her parent's marriage. That was normal to her, not the easygoing, relaxed atmosphere that Heather and Joe enjoyed. That was something she needed to think about. She wished she were able to talk to her counselor, but that was impossible. She was not going back to San Francisco, not now when she had come this far. This is where she would stay, and like Heather and Joe, 'deal with whatever comes.'

Chapter 18

They turned on Dennis Street and parked the van where they had parked before. A woman got out of a car and stood while they were getting out of the van. She's sizing me up, Mara thought. She put a smile on her face and extending her hand, she introduced herself and Heather to her potential new landlord.

"Hi Mara, I'm Lori, and the apartment is ready for you to see."

"I can't wait," replied Mara.

Lori led them up the stairs to the front of the building talking as she walked. "You will have three entrances, this one is the formal entrance, and you can also get to the apartment from the underground garage and the back door. I pay for cable and the garbage. You are responsible for your own power; I take care of the gas heating. You also have an assigned spot in the garage. I also have a washer and dryer down there for the tenants to use."

They entered the foyer and Heather gushed, "Look at this wallpaper, and all of this natural woodwork, it's gorgeous."

They stopped at the apartment marked A, Lori inserted the key and turned the handle. The charm of the apartment stopped Mara in her tracks. It was beautiful. It felt like her home. She knew it was an apartment that she would feel comfortable in, and she hadn't seen the rest of it yet.

Lori was saying, "The carpeting is new and the window treatments and blinds go with the. My handyman lives right down the street on Dennis and he is right on the spot to take care of any problems you might have."

Lori led them through an arched doorway into a small dining room. It had a coat closet and it was huge. She would have plenty of storage space, even if she didn't have anything to store yet.

"This is a galley kitchen, no room for a table, but plenty of cabinets and the appliances are new. I even have a microwave in here that stays with the apartment."

They followed Lori through the hallway toward the bath and bedroom.

"Oh look Mara, it's a built in bookcase. Don't you just love it?

"I do. Lori, if I receive word on my job tomorrow, I'll take it."

" Ok, you have my phone number, we'll get together to sign the lease, and you can move in whenever you want."

"I'll show you out the back door and the underground garage so you'll be familiar with it, there's a remote for the garage door and only the tenants have one."

Heather said, "Mara this is just adorable and I can picture it decorated and I know where to get the decorations."

Mara had to laugh; her best friend was so excited. "Do we need to go shopping today? I don't have word on my job yet and I'm a little worried about taking it and buying furnishings until I hear from Millikin."

"Of course we are going shopping. I am that confident that you are going to get that job, and this apartment is perfect for you. Close to work, and close to me too."

Lori let them out of the apartment and made sure Mara had her cell phone number so she could call if she decided to take the apartment.

"I'll hold it for you till tomorrow night, that way if you get your job, it will be here waiting for you. I'd be happy to have you as my new tenant. Talk to you soon."

"Let's get started. I can hardly wait. Where should we go first?"

"You know the area; I'll just go where you go."

Giggling Heather jumped in the van, "I know just where to go first. Will you be buying new or second hand?"

Mara thought for a moment and replied, "I think I'll buy a good bed, an inexpensive living room set, and try to find a used dining room table. There are all the household goods I will need also."

"Well, I think I can help you out with some of that. Joe bought me a new set of dishes and new set of pans about two months ago, and I put the old ones down in the basement to save back for a garage sale. You are welcome to them, and it will make Joe happy with more room in the basement. I'm such a packrat. I can't bear to throw anything away."

Chapter 19

They headed East on Route 36 and stopped at a mostly uninhabited strip mall. Heather led her to a bedding store. "We've bought from here; they're reasonable and have free delivery. I think we can find you a bedroom set, and there's another store in Mt. Zion that carries living room furniture as well. Come on, let's take a look."

Wandering around the store, Mara spied a honey colored country pine queen-size bed, with a matching dresser and bedside table. "Oh I love this. It's in my price range too."

The salesclerk approached them and Mara negotiated with him to hold it until the next evening until she was sure she would take the apartment. Of course, it depended on if Millikin offered her the Public Relations position.

"Ok where to next? Mt. Zion? Brothers run both stores and you'll get a good deal with him too. I'm sure he'll work with you about holding it till you get an answer from the University."

"Sounds good to me, I don't need a table yet, I can eat off a TV tray so I can postpone that till I get my first paycheck."

Driving to the furniture store in Mt. Zion, they laughed about why one city would have two Super Wal-Marts. The best friends were falling into the special relationship they enjoyed while they were growing up. Mara felt relaxed and happy. The job was hers she felt it in her heart. It seemed perfect, and she began to feel like things were too good to be true. It was hard for her to allow herself to be happy, she was trying to get past the feelings she was always waiting for the other shoe to drop. She gave a little sigh; it is good for me to have such an outgoing and fun loving friend. Heather reflected joy in her every mood and optimism flowed out of her eyes and body.

Finding the furniture store, they went in, and started browsing. Mara spotted a country blue sofa with matching love seat, she knew would work in the living room. She chose a couple of end tables and they put them on hold until Thursday night as well. This brother was just as nice as the first one at the bedding store.

"Mara the TV in your room can be yours for as long as you want to use it. They have a good cable service here, and Lori said basic cable is part of the rent."

Getting in the van, they drove to Wal-Mart to buy some basic linen. She would have time to pick up other items, as she needed them. She'd start out simple. She didn't like clutter and she tended to travel light, in case she needed to pack and go again. She would sign the lease for a year, but after the year was over, she would reevaluate her life. If moving back to Illinois would bring back her fears, and insecurities, she needed to be flexible enough to move somewhere else.

Mara had a cart full of household supplies, linens, and cleaning supplies. If things didn't work out, they were all items Heather could use. They loaded up the van after checking out and Heather said. "There's one more place I want to take you, a place where you can pick up used books, and whimsical decorations that you won't find in a Wal-Mart. One of a kind items, I know you'll love it."

Driving back to Decatur, Mara tried to get her bearings so she'd be able to get around the city on her own. Main and Main crossed each other and that was the center of town. I'm going to pull up a map from the internet and print it, it will come in handy, she thought.

"Here we are. I know you'll just love this place. I know you like to read, so maybe you'll find some good used books for that built in bookshelf. Novel Ideas is a treasure trove of used books."

The storeowner greeted them as they entered and invited them to take all the time they needed to look around. Mara found a Thomas Kincaid sun catcher with the Golden Gate Bridge pictured on it. It was a little pricey, but it would help her to hang on to the tools she learned from her therapy sessions. She could do her visual meditation with the sun catcher and place herself back into the peaceful setting she once lived in.

She bought a few books, a couple of them on local history written by local authors, and a biography of Abe Lincoln. Her favorite teacher had made the 16th president come alive for her and she wanted to read more. He was her hero; he had risen from a poor background to become first a great lawyer, then the President of the United States. It reminded her, no matter what you began; you have control of the ending. She needed to remember she was in control of her own destiny now. She needed to hang on to the confidence that she felt when she had come back to Illinois. She needed to remain in control of her emotions and not allow herself to slip back into old patterns. You can do this; you are strong, capable, and successful. You are someone to be proud of. She gave herself more positive self-talk; she felt she needed the boost to help her through the day.

Taking their purchases back to the car, Mara handed Heather a sack. "Here, this is a present for you. I saw you admiring it and I think it will look great hanging on your front porch."

Opening the sack, Heather found the wind chimes she had admired in the little shop.

"Mara, thank you so much, you didn't have to do that. However, I'm glad you did, I love it and know right were to hang it. It will go on the front porch near the door so I can hear the chimes in the living room. What a soothing sound they make."

"Consider it a hostess gift for allowing me the privilege to stay with your family. I feel so blessed by your friendship." For the second time that day, the two friends hugged.

"Well then, I think it might be time for us to head back to Illiopolis, pick up the kids, and eat our casserole and rest. We've shopped till we're ready to drop."

They drove back in compatible silence. It was a sure sign that Heather was tired if she was too tired to talk.

Joe had already picked up the kids and had the casserole in the oven when they arrived home. Baths finished and JJ and Melody would be ready for bed after dinner.

"Heather you have a keeper in Joe. You're so lucky."

"I know, he's wonderful to me and a great Father. We have a perfect life and I'm so happy."

The evening ended with Joe and JJ playing Chutes and Ladders while Heather and Mara chased little Melody around the house while she pretended to run away. Her giggles were so cute and they enchanted Mara.

Soon, it was bedtime for the children, and Mara decided her day had been tiring and decided to head to bed early. She would work a little on her laptop, research Milliken's website and check out the website for Decatur too. She wanted to be familiar with the University's program and find out what else in Decatur had to offer. She soon found there was plenty to do in Decatur, and she thought she would have fun exploring the city. She found listings for nice restaurants, the North Fork museum and the Decatur Arts Council.

Soon, her eyes began to grow heavy. Turning off her laptop, she was soon asleep. That night, no dreams troubled her slumber.

Chapter 20

Thursday morning Mara awoke to the sound of rain pounding on the roof. She jumped out of bed, determined to make it a good day no matter the weather. She rushed through her shower singing her favorite Gretchen Wilson song. She was in a good mood, she felt confident, and today she felt she was ready for anything. Her cell phone rang as she was drying her hair, when she answered, she found her Mother on the line.

"Mara, I just wanted to confirm that you are still coming to dinner tomorrow night. I told your Father you were in town, he's agitated, but he's prepared. Come on over about six, dinner will be ready. I have a customer now, so good-bye and we will see you tomorrow evening."

I couldn't get a word in edgewise, but at least I am going, Mara thought. She was dressing when the phone rang a second time.

"Hello."

"Mara, this is Carol Mathews calling from Millikin University. I am calling to offer you the job if you want it. I spoke to Dean Hall, showed him your resume and references. He has a favorable impression of you. If you want to come in this morning, we will get all the necessary paperwork filled out and you can plan to start work on Monday morning."

"That's wonderful." Mara exclaimed. I can be there around ten o'clock this morning if that would be a good time."

"Sure come on in, I'll show you around and let you see your office and you'll be able to meet some of your co-workers. In fact, if you plan to have lunch here, I'll be able to introduce you to most of our faculty."

"That sounds wonderful Carol. I will be there at ten. Thanks for calling and I am happy to accept the job."

She skipped to the top of the stairs, "Heather. I got the job."

Heather run up the stairs giggling, "Silly, I knew you would. Now you need to call Lori and tell her you want the apartment, and arrange to get your furniture delivered. Is there anything I can do?"

"Nope not a thing, I'm going in to fill out the paperwork and meet some of the people I'll be working with. I'll be staying for lunch with Carol so I won't be home until later this afternoon. Why don't we go celebrate my new job? Didn't you say there was a good steakhouse in Decatur? It's my treat to you and Joe for allowing me to stay with you this week. Of course, I expect JJ and Melody to come along too."

Mara was out of breath, with a million plans whirling in her mind. Her call from Carol drove her Mother's phone call out of her head. "Wait, Heather, Mother called to say she and Father are expecting me for dinner at six tomorrow evening.

She didn't sound happy about it, but since I told her I would just show up on her doorstep, she gave in and told Father I was in town."

"Well, I hope everything goes ok for you tomorrow night. Remember, you're a different person now. You are mature, successful, and confident. Don't let others get you down by their attitudes." She gave her a quick hug; "I'll need to hustle to get JJ to school. See you tonight, I'll tell Joe we are going to Texas Roadhouse, that's his favorite place to eat."

With that, she was gone and soon Mara heard her going out the door. She took her time dressing in a conservative pantsuit, put her make up on, and decided to wear her hair up today. She took a last look in the mirror. You're all right girl, you can do this, and you WILL be strong."

Getting in the car, she called Lori and asked her when she could sign the lease for the apartment. Now that she had a job and the fact she was moving into her new apartment made her giddy with excitement. She didn't mind being alone, she had been alone most of her life anyway. She knew she would be content. She thought, maybe I will get a kitten to keep me company. Yes, that's a good idea.

Mara arranged to meet Lori at three that afternoon to sign the lease and pay her first months rent and deposit. Raining or not, this was going to be a great day. She felt a load lifting from her shoulders. She was doing the right thing after all. The job, the apartment, everything was falling into place for her.

She was a little early for her appointment so she took a walk around the campus. It was beautiful; brick buildings, beautiful flowerbeds, and it looked so peaceful. She knew she'd be happy here. She looked across Main Street and the house on the corner had a sign on it that said, "Millikin Alumni Association." She knew she would be spending some time over there as well as in her office. The possibilities were endless and she whispered a prayer of thanks for everything.

The rain was still falling but with her umbrella and fashionable boots, she didn't worry about the weather. Her hair would still be fine since she was wearing it up today. She found the Athletic center, and knew she would make use of the facilities. She didn't want to get flabby from lack of exercise. She had exercised regularly in San Francisco and it always helped her mood. She peeked inside the library. It was a beautiful building, well stocked with both books and computers. This was a good University, privately funded so she knew tuition would be high. If she got the chance, she was going to take a class or two, but not before her new job was running smoothly.

Heading back to the administration building she walked with a purposeful stride. This was her niche, she knew this work, and she was confident she'd be good at this job.

Beth, the receptionist greeted her, asking her to have a seat while she told Carol she was here. No one was sitting at the other desk, but the nameplate said Sam. That didn't help her. Sam could be either male or female. Oh well, she knew she'd eventually get to know everyone. She had to fight against the shyness that still sometimes threatened to overcome her.

"Hi Mara," said Carol, "Follow me. I want you to meet the Dean."

The Dean's office was furnished simply with a few family pictures on his desk and his awards and diplomas on the wall.

"Mara Conley, I'd like to introduce you to Dean Gary Hall." Dean Hall stood and extended his hand to her. "I am happy to meet you; I am impressed with your resume. I have talked to a couple of your references, and they gave you nothing but praise for the work you did for them. Welcome to the team."

He was smiling and Mara noticed a slight gap in his two front teeth. His gray hair needed a haircut, but he was the image of an academic. His glasses sat on the end of his nose, he had a twinkle in his eye, and she liked him immediately.

"I'm happy to be joining the team. I hope I'll be able to make a contribution to the University."

"I'm sure you will. You made a good impression on Carol and her recommendation means a lot. She is a workaholic boss, but good at what she does"

"Really Dean Hall, you'll have Mara scared of me before she even starts. We're going to my office to sign all the forms that need signed, then I'll show her the office she'll occupy and then we're having lunch in the faculty lunchroom."

"Sounds like a good plan, Mara, I am looking forward to working with you. I understand you will start working on Monday."

"Yes sir, I am looking forward to it." Offering her hand once more, she shook it firmly and they left the office.

Carol said, "He is good to work for, generous to a fault and the students and faculty all love him. You'll like working for him and I hope for me too."

They walked down a short hall just past Carol's office and into an office a little smaller then Carol's, but equipped tastefully, with a computer, printer, and scanner on the desk. They have it all ready for me. I'll just bring in a few plants to make it feel more like home, she thought.

"Anything you need, you can ask Sam or Beth for, Sam only comes in for a half day in the afternoon, she just had a new baby but we begged her to work part-time. She will be your personal assistant, and if you need more help, Beth is always willing to do whatever she's handed."

"I'm sure I'll have all I need. I'm self-reliant, but always glad for a helping hand if the going gets tough."

"You'll have several busy times during the year, but, it's ordinary work. You'll interact with faculty, students, alumni, and parents. It can be demanding, but I have every confidence that you'll be able to handle the job."

After signing all the necessary forms, they headed over to the dining hall. Menu on the wall said it was meat loaf today and it smelled delicious. There was a quiet hubbub where some of the faculty had already found a seat and were chatting with friends. They looked up with interest when Carol and Mara walked in.

"Hey everyone, this is Mara Conley, she's our new Public Relations person. Drop by and say hello when you're finished eating."

They went through the line, picked up their lunch, and sat at a table near the center of the room. Carol wasn't taking any chances that people wouldn't be able to meet their new co-worker. Faculty members stopping by the table to introduce themselves interrupted her meal several times. She knew she'd never remember all the names, but she worked hard at trying to put their faces and names together. She knew it would take awhile, but names were one of her strong points. She made mental notes to herself to help associate a name with a face. She enjoyed her lunch, and thanked Carol as they were preparing to leave.

"I'll see you on Monday," said Mara. "I need to go and sign the lease for my apartment now, and arrange to have some furniture delivered. I'm hoping to move in this weekend."

"Sure, enjoy your weekend and we'll set you to work on Monday morning. Hours are eight to five, but we can be flexible, you'll be working outside those hours anyway during our busy times."

Chapter 21

She drove down Main Street to the apartment to meet Lori. She was anxious to see it again, hoping it would look as good to her today as it did yesterday. Lori was waiting in her car and when Mara stepped out of her car, so did she. "I didn't know what you'd be driving today, you were in your friend's minivan yesterday, and I didn't want to miss you."

"I am just a few minutes late, and I apologize for that. I was meeting with my new employers at Millikin."

"No problem, let's take a walk through the apartment again, then we'll sign the lease and I'll give you your keys."

The apartment seemed roomy and looked even better today then it did yesterday. She was going to be happy here, she could feel it.

Mara signed the lease, paid the deposit and first months rent paid then Lori handed her the keys to her apartment and the remote for the garage.

"If you need anything, just give me a call. My handyman Dan lives across the street and he's always willing to do whatever needs done. Have a good weekend, bye."

Mara sat down on the living room floor and called the two furniture stores. She arranged for the furniture to be delivered the next morning. Tomorrow will be a big day, moving, and going to my parents for dinner. You can handle it Mara, you know you can. Keep cool and don't let circumstances rattle you.

Good advice, she just hoped she was able to do what she was telling herself to do.

She ran down to the shopping center, picked up a few essentials, and took them back to put in her cupboards and refrigerator. Now she felt better, she was making it her place. She would ask Heather where to find a good flower shop so she could buy some plants. She loved plants, and the many windows in the apartment would give them plenty of sunshine. She knew she would need to get a small stereo; she couldn't live without the soothing noise of her music. She seldom watched TV, but she did enjoy watching old movies and tonight was her one night for watching her three favorite shows; Survivor, CSI and Without a Trace. It was the only night she enjoyed watched TV. She had her books, and she dabbled in writing some. She would have some time for that. She would miss Heather, Joe, and the kids, but she would still see them often, and there was always the phone.

It was going on four o'clock and she knew she needed to get on the road. It pleased Mara to be able to take her friends to their favorite restaurant, enjoy their company for at least one more night. She would miss JJ and Melody; they had already won a permanent spot in her heart. I've always loved children, and these two are so special.

Everyone was waiting on her when she arrived at Heather's. JJ came and threw his arms around her giving her a big hug, "I love Texas Roadhouse," he said. Melody was jabbering away saying "Ye haw." They were so excited. Mara was happy to celebrate with special friends, and she was a little hungry. She hadn't eaten much of her lunch; she was too busy meeting her co-workers.

They all piled into the minivan and started the drive to Decatur. The kids sat in the backseat in their car seats and Heather popped a movie in the DVD player for them. They each wore a set of earphones, so Heather, Joe and Mara were able to talk. The meal was delicious and the conversation lighthearted and they enjoyed the time spent together and then treated themselves to delicious chocolate brownie sundae dessert. The kids especially like it when the servers all did the dance to 'Cotton-Eyed Joe'. They all clapped and hooted, with Melody saying, "Ye haw." Over and again.

"We'll hear that for days now," said Heather shaking her head and smiling.

Getting back into the van, the kids put their headphones on, but ten minutes away from the restaurant, they were asleep. It was so quiet, just a comfortable stillness among friends.

Joe spoke up, "Mara, please be careful if you have to work after dark. If you are the only one going out of a building, be sure to call campus security. The University hired them to take care of their students. You can't be too careful. Always watch to make sure no one is following you home, and don't pull over on a quiet deserted street, not even for a police car. They will follow you to a lit and occupied area and always make sure they show their ID."

"Joe you're such a worrywart! However, thanks for all the good advice just the same, and I'll remember what you said. I'm going to like my new neighborhood."

They drove quietly, Mara lost in thought, wondering what tomorrow would bring when she would meet with her parents. She didn't want to get her hopes up, her Mom had been cool, and she knew that she was different when she was around her husband. She thought don't worry about that tonight, just enjoy the evening with your friends, don't borrow trouble Mara.

She said goodnight to Joe and Heather after they had tucked their children into bed. "I'm going to have another emotional day tomorrow. I think I'll head to bed."

"Thanks for the wonderful meal," Joe said

"Thanks from me too. We had a great time, it's a treat for us as we don't often go out to eat, and the kids enjoyed themselves. They think it's so cool to throw peanut shells on the floor."

" I haven't been around children much since I was a baby-sitter, but I do love your little ones. Have a good evening, good-night"

Mara went to her room, prepared for bed, and sighed when she finally hit the pillow. It had been a long exhausting day but she was happy. She went to sleep planning on how she would arrange her furniture.

She was walking in a long hallway, she could hear a woman crying but couldn't tell which room the cries were coming from. She opened each door as she came to it; the hallway seemed to go on forever. The cries were getting louder, she thought she was getting closer, she heard a new cry, that of a newborn baby. She could hear a man's voice and he was screaming. What was he saying? She tried to get closer so she could hear, but just when she was beginning to hear the words, she saw a door swing open and a man hurry down the hall. She couldn't tell who it was, but could tell by the way that he was stalking down the hall he wasn't happy. Still she heard the cries of the woman and the cries of the baby. She went to the door where the man had come from. Opening it just a crack she looked in. There was the woman, she was holding a baby, and by the color of the blanket, it must be a girl. The folds of the baby blanket hid the woman's face and she was sobbing her heart out. "How could he go behind my back and name you Mara. He knew I wanted to call you Catherine." The woman looked up, it was her own Mother, and the baby had to be her. She ran back into the hallway just as the man turned and gave one final look. It was her Father.

She awoke with her heart thudding in her chest. She thought about the dream, and what it meant. The only way to find out was to confront her parents. She didn't want to hurt them, but she had 26 years of hurt built up and she needed to get to the root of the problem. She slept little the rest of the night.

Chapter 22

The next morning she was groggy and felt achy. She went in to take a shower to try to refresh and wake her up. She had errands to run today, phone calls to make to get the power in her name, and then the dinner with her parents tonight. She tried to dispel the feelings of anxiety she was having. She practiced her deep breathing techniques, and let the hot water pound her body until she felt calmer. Today was not the day to fall apart.

Dressing in jeans and a 49'rs sweatshirt, she felt better prepared for the day. She wanted to be at her apartment when the furniture arrived and take over what few belongings Heather had given her, and what she had bought. She knew she would need to do more shopping once she moved in.

The delicious smell of bacon and eggs drifted up the stairs and Mara realized she was hungry. She would need her strength for this day, with the physical and emotional demands it would make on her. Walking in to the kitchen she greeted Heather and Joe, Melody was smiling and waving her arms at her, JJ jumped up to give her a hug. I'm going to miss this family when I move out. I didn't know you could be so close to someone and love them as I do JJ and Melody.

Heather said, "Today is the big day. Is there anything I can do to help you? I have errands to run this morning and then I can take Melody to my Mom's and be available for you."

"Really there isn't much to do other then take over the few household items I have and wait for the furniture. I can make the phone call to put the power in my name on my cell phone and take care of those chores. I think I will just try to put some clothes away when the bedroom furniture comes, and place the furniture in the living room where I want it. I want to be calm when I visit my parents tonight. I need to be calm and collected. Do you mind if I stay one more night in your guestroom?"

"Of course you can, I want to hear all about your day and your visit with your parents anyway. We'll make some popcorn and talk, if we run out of subjects to talk about we can watch a movie."

"Like that would ever happen," Joe laughed. "Well girls, I need to start my shift, so I'll see you later." He bent over to kiss JJ and tousle his hair. Melody held her arms up for a hug which he gave her, then went to the sink to wipe the toast crumbs off his uniform.

"Bye Joe, have a good day." Said Mara,

"Bye sweetheart, I will see you later tonight. I love you, be careful." Heather kissed him and hugged him tight. He waved to them as he walked out the door.

"I always hate to see him go in the morning, the thought scares me about what might happen during the day with the job he is in."

"I can't imagine how you must feel. I would worry too," said Mara.

"Come on JJ it's time for you to go to school, and Melody you are running errands with Mommy today. Mara, you have my cell phone, if you need some help or just a little extra courage, give me a call." She hugged her friend and hurried the children out the door.

I am more comfortable giving and getting hugs now. Just a few days with this wonderful family and I am already different. She thought. It feels so wonderful to be close to someone. I could get to enjoy this family business.

She surprised herself at the thought. She planned on never getting married and having a family, and here she was longing for one. Not like the family that she had grown up with, but the one like Heather and Joe enjoyed.

She tidied up the kitchen and then went to pack her few belongings and put her clothes back in her suitcases, and garment bag. Joe said he would bring the TV over tomorrow and she thought she would go buy a DVD player, so she could watch some of her favorite movies. She knew there was a Video Store in the shopping center, and she liked the idea of curling up on the sofa enjoying her peace and solitude. She liked being alone, she knew she would be fine. Heather had given her a small CD player, so she would have the comfort of her music.

Packing the car took nearly an hour. When finished, she drove to Main Street Mall to pick up some cinnamon rolls and homemade bread she could eat while waiting for her furniture. Not healthy, but good comfort food, and that's what she needed today for sure. She waved at her Mother but didn't stop in the shop.

She was tense today, her muscles knotted in her neck, and shoulders made her uncomfortable. She knew it was just the tension of tonight's dinner with her parents. She was happy making a new home, decorating it in her own style, and making it comfortable for her. It would take awhile but the furniture and decor would fall together and it would become home to her.

She entered the apartment through the entrance in the garage and looked around. It was a little stark and she knew she needed to buy some valances to brighten up the windows. She wanted to add colorful wall decorations and some plants. She longed for the apartment to be hers, with her personality showing through.

She heard a truck pull up and found that some of her furniture had arrived. It was her bedroom furniture. Wonderful I'll get my bedroom done for sure even though I'm not spending the night, she thought. Mara directed the men to where she wanted her dresser and bed placed. When they left, she hung up her clothes and put the lingerie in the dresser drawers. Since she had only bought a dresser, she would need to invest in a mirror to put in her bedroom. She wasn't vain, but she did like to check her appearance before she left for work. She needed to make a list; she needed cleaning supplies for sure and some items that she just plain wanted. She would find her way to the mall tomorrow and work on her apartment over the weekend. She was positive it would be neat and orderly when she went to work on Monday morning.

She was unpacking the dishes Heather had given her when she heard the other truck pull up. Good, the rest of the furniture is here. The furniture made a huge difference in the feel of the apartment. It was beginning to feel more like home. She couldn't wait to add the little touches that would make it hers.

Puttering around, arranging the kitchen, and munching on a cinnamon roll, she laughed out loud how pleased she was. Putting her home together felt so good, it was relaxing for her. She had her favorite CD in the CD player and she sang with Tim McGraw. We carry on; yes, that's what she was doing. She was carrying on with her life. She intended to take it slow and easy and let events unfold in their own time.

It was midafternoon before she knew it. She needed to get back to clean up and get ready to go to her parents. Again, she found her muscles knotting up. Breathe, long deep breaths, she told herself. She locked the apartment and headed back to Illiopolis, this time she didn't sing as she was driving. She spent her time thinking and trying to discover the meaning of her recurring dream. She shook her head, and then laughed at the sight of her face in the rearview mirror. She looked stressed and she worked on relaxing and letting go of the tensions that bound her in knots. Breathe Mara, deep breaths, and let your mind wander to the beach. You can do this.

Once in Illiopolis, she decided to stop at the Bakery in Johnson's Market for a dessert to take home as well as the fresh bread she had bought from Lana this morning. She was checking out when someone came up behind her and touched her lightly on the arm. Startled, she turned around to see a woman who was vaguely familiar to her.

"So you are back." The woman smirked. "Jerry said he saw you and how wonderful you look. I see the same person, just dressed a little nicer. Well good luck around here, you'll find not much has changed. With that, Jerry Lowe's sister turned and stalked out the door.

Mara could feel her face burning, she was the one person who bullied her most in school, the one she wanted most to impress, and there she went. I just stood there and took it, just like high school. Didn't I learn anything with all that therapy?

She paid for the dessert she had chosen and a few staples she had picked up for her apartment and walked out the door. The words from her childhood taunted her as she walked to her car, "No one loves me, everyone hates me, guess I'll go eat worms."

She hadn't thought of those words for over five years and suddenly, here they were teasing her mind, gnawing at her self-confidence. She didn't need this, right before this evening with her parents. Apprehension started washing over her in waves. She had to get a grip; she couldn't arrive at her parents nearly in the midst of a panic attack. She sat in her car, breathing deep cleansing breaths, making a conscious effort to relax every part of her muscles.

When her breathing was calmer and the anxiety began to ebb, she closed her eyes and imagined her secret place. She was in a beach cottage, with the sand shimmering under a bright sun, the waves gently lapping against the shore. She could smell the hibiscus blossoms in the air and feel the gentle breeze as it fluttered her hair, and caressed her cheek. Serenity filled her and she began to calm down. Yes, you can do it; you are in control of your body. Circumstances may not be in your control, but you can control how you react to them.

With those encouraging words, she started the car and drove the few blocks to her childhood home.

Chapter 23

She parked in the driveway and looked around. The house looked rundown and neglected. When her Father was healthy, he made sure the house and the yard were immaculate. When he wasn't working at the plant, he was outside working around the house, puttering in the garage, or doing yard work. She knew it had to be tough on him to sit all-day in a wheelchair, barely able to feed or take care of himself. She felt a twinge of guilt that she hadn't been there to help when her Dad got sick. Her Mother had needed her help and she hadn't been here for her. No. You did what you had to do. You've grown stronger and you are different now. You'll carry on just like your favorite song. Even when life comes undone, you carry on.

She stepped out of the car and walked to the front door. No decorations hung there, something unusual for her Mother, but she did have her hands full. It must be a full-time job taking care of her Father and running the salon too. A shiver went down her spine as she reached for the doorbell. This used to be her home, but it had never felt comfortable here. She hadn't been happy here, she knew that for sure. She could only remember unhappy memories from her childhood. She tried and tried to think of happy times in her childhood, but the few she must have had wouldn't come to her mind.

Her Mother answered the door, wearing a pair of black slacks and dark gray blouse. The tantalizing aroma from the pork roast met Mara as she stepped in the door.

"I brought dessert, I remember Father having a love of chocolate, and I bought us a double chocolate fudge cake."

There was no welcoming look in her Mother's eyes; just sadness and a sigh escaped her lips as if she were accepting the unavoidable. Tonight she looked old, and the change in her Father's appearance shocked Mara. His wheelchair made the small room look even smaller but he still sat at the head of the table. His face was gaunt with one side of his face drooping and one arm lying useless in his lap. He looked at her with the same glare that he always wore when looking at her. The tension in the air was thick, Mara started to panic. Could she do this? Try to reconcile with her parents, resurrect the past, and get past it? She didn't know, but she knew she had to try. Her future depended on it, as well as her happiness. She needed her adult life to be free of the past, and the little girl in her could finally enjoy her freedom. Free to be who God meant her to be.

"Hello Father," she walked over and kissed him lightly on the cheek. "I know it's been a longtime and I'm sorry you aren't well."

His stare continued to make her uneasy. She put a smile on her face and headed toward the kitchen. "I brought you some chocolate cake, I remember that's your favorite dessert." Still there was no response from the lifeless form that had the face of her Father. The cold stare penetrated her soul. She wanted to run, to escape, and flee as she had done the night of graduation. She couldn't, she knew that but this was going to be harder then she thought. Her Mother followed her into the kitchen.

"He doesn't say much, and if he does speak it's not clear. I can't always understand him and that makes him even more frustrated. I don't know how he'll act tonight." She gathered bowls of steaming vegetables and the sliced pork roast and headed toward the dining room. Mara picked up a couple of dishes and followed her Mother.

They sat down at the table, sitting in the same place they used to sit. It was eerie, she felt like she was ten years old again. They bowed their heads, and her mother asked the blessing on the food, instead of Father. He mumbled with the prayer and his Amen was understandable at the end.

At first, they passed the food and ate quietly, and then Mara began to ask questions about people she had known, children she had baby-sat for, and some of the elderly people she had known from the Church. Seeing the headstones of people she'd known as a child made her sad.

What bothered her most were the stories of two young men that she baby-sat for when they were little. One teenager had committed suicide by lying across the railroad tracks just outside town. The other one was even sadder, and tears came to her eyes as her Mother related the story.

"Jason was a good kid, popular in high school and a top athlete. He graduated and went into the Air Force. He loved it, and was happy to be serving his country. One day his Mom and Dad got a call that he was sick and would soon be home from overseas to consult with Doctors at Bethesda Hospital. What they found was horrible, he had an advanced form of cancer, and it had spread to his liver already. His parents brought him home to take care of him, he traveled back and forth between Illinois and Washington D.C. for treatments. His Mom searched the Internet for anything that might be able to help him…even experimental drugs. Finally, with the chemo not helping and just making him weaker he decided to stop treatments. He put his finances in order, wrote down exactly what he wanted for his funeral services, and continued to live his life. He shot pool with his Dad, adored and played with his niece, and was a good friend to all who knew him. I liked him especially because he would talk to young and old alike, it didn't make any difference to him. He was able to live on his own for a short time and went on with his life. He went to one final Christmas party with his friends. After the party they took him the hospital. Christmas morning, with his family gathered round him, he died."

"Oh no," said Mara, "He was such a sweet little boy, and I enjoyed baby-sitting for him, his sister Amber and brother Ryan."

"The funeral was huge, they had to have it in the school gym to get everyone in that wanted to go to the visitation. They had a beautiful collection of his pictures from the time he was a baby, through his high school athletic activities, and when he was playing pool with his Dad. His best friends spoke at the service, because he had asked them to before he died. There wasn't a dry eye in the whole place. Illiopolis loved Jason."

"I am sorry to hear that, I'll stop by their bar and tell them how sorry I am."

Mara's Father mumbled something and started motioning his wife to do something for him. She had already cut his meat for him and he did a good job of eating. Thankfully, the stroke had affected the side that wasn't his dominant side.

"What do you want dear? Would you like more gravy on your meat?" He shook his head yes and she poured some gravy from the gravy boat over his meat and potatoes. He didn't have an easy time with his corn, so he shoveled it into his mashed potatoes and ate them together. Mara glanced at him, not once did she catch him looking at her. If was as if she was invisible. Typical, he did the same as it always had been the whole time I was growing up; Mara thought, but still, it bothered her.

"Let me push Father in to the living room and turn on TV for him, then we will clear the table. We can have dessert before I have to put him to bed."

With that, she spoke to him gently and rolled him to the other room. He was mumbling something, but Mara was not close enough to catch even a word or two of what he was saying. She started gathering the dishes, it all seemed so automatic, and it felt as if she never left. Force of habit made her get up and clear the table; she had the dishes gathered, and some in the dishwasher when her Mother came in.

"He's agitated, keeps trying to say something, but I can't understand what he's saying. That makes him even more frustrated." She sighed. "I don't know what to do any more."

"Mother, why does Father look at me the way he does? Why doesn't he love me? Why do you treat me different when he isn't around? I don't understand, and I need to. I also need to know family history for medical reasons. I have an eye disease that is genetic, and I want to know which side of the family it comes from. Won't you help me please?"

Barbara stiffened and stopped wiping the counter with the dishcloth. "Why do you have to have all those answers? Can't you just leave it alone? It's all in the past now, and what is in the past needs to stay in the past."

"No, I've sensed all my life that something is different about me, about the circumstances of my birth. I've been having this dream, always the same dream, with you crying in the hospital, and Father leaving the room walking away from both of us. Is it just a dream? On the other hand, is it something buried in my memory that is surfacing and making me demand some answers? There is still my eye disease; Retina Pigmentosis is a disease only one parent can pass on. Sure, it can skip a few generations, but why don't I remember anyone in the family suffering from it? You have to help me." Then she started to cry. "All I've ever wanted from you and Father is your love, and you're both still holding that back from me. I have to know why."

Her Mother wrung the dishcloth out, and turned to another cabinet. "Discovering I was pregnant was a surprise to us. Our life style didn't include a new baby. We thought we'd never have our own baby. You were a shock to us, that's all. We were too old to have a child then, we didn't know how to be a Mommy and Daddy. Can't you just leave it at that?"

"I would if I felt that was all there was to it, but I don't believe that for a moment. I have learned too much in the few days I have been back. You didn't take me out of the house for months; you didn't even take me to Church to be dedicated. That is so unlike you and Father, it doesn't make sense."

"Mara, can we please not talk about this anymore tonight? I'm tired and have a bad headache and your Father hasn't been good today. I need to go check on him. Please cut us all a piece of cake and bring it to the living room. That's all I am going to say about the past right now." With those parting words, she left the kitchen.

Mara stood at the sink looking out the kitchen window to the bare cornfield beyond the back of the property. She caught a glimpse of red dots, and realized she was looking at a deer, his eyes reflecting red in the moonlight. She pulled three cake plates out of the cupboard, cut each of them a piece of cake, and walked toward the living room. What a bust, I've spent an uncomfortable evening and no new news either.

Chapter 24

The early evening news was on when she walked into the living room carrying three plates of sliced chocolate cake. Suddenly, her eyes jumped to the TV screen. The camera was showing the outside the State Capitol building. The TV cameras focused on State Police cars, one in particular with the door open and a pool of blood seeping out of the car door.

The reporter was talking, "Two State Troopers responded to a call from the Capitol building about a hostage crisis. A newly divorced husband has barged in and is demanding his wife meet him outside. There had been a nasty custody battle and the Father had lost visitation rights with his children because of his violent behavior. The word we have now is, one State Trooper wounded, and the other one could be dead. The man, identified as Harold Brand is still holding his wife and two of her co-workers hostage. He is threatening to kill them and himself before he will surrender. The names of the two officers are being withheld until notification of relatives. We will continue to watch this story and bring you any new breaking news."

The TV screen went back to the News Anchors who were shaking their heads and wondering about the state of the world. Mara thought of Heather, "I need to call Heather, her husband is a State Trooper and he was working the Springfield area today." She walked into the hallway to place the call to Heather's home.

Someone finally picked up the phone, but it wasn't Heather. An unfamiliar voice asked who was calling. Mara explained who she was, and asked to speak to Heather. The voice on the other end introduced herself as a friend of Heather's. Her daughter went to school with JJ, and then she explained why she was there.

"Heather has reason to believe that Joe is one of the State Trooper caught in the stand off at the Capitol building. She thought she recognized his car on the news, and his superior just called asking her to come to Springfield right away. I live two houses down, so she called me, I'll stay here with JJ and Melody, but if you can come here and drive her to Springfield, I think it would be better for her. I am afraid for her to drive in her state of mind, and she turned down the offer for a Patrol car pick her up."

"I'll be right there, I'm only a few minutes away. Don't let her go till I get there."

Rushing back to the living room, she explained what was happening to her Mother and prepared to leave. She went over to kiss her Father on the cheek, he ducked his head, and she caught the side of his head instead. Walking over to her Mother, she held her by the shoulders, gave her a kiss on the cheek, and said, "We aren't finished here yet. I will have my answers one way or another." She turned and walked out the door.

The ride to Heather and Joe's was quick, she pushed the car as fast as she dared on a city street, and pulled in the driveway in record time. Jumping out of the car, she ran to the front door, just as it was opening and Heather came running out.

"Let's go," said Heather. "I have to get there as soon as I can."

"Is Joe one of the officers involved?"

"His superior said 'maybe' but Joe would have called me on his cell phone so I wouldn't worry, and he hasn't called. I'm afraid Mara, I am so afraid." She buried her head in her hands and Mara could hear the muffled sobs and whispered words of prayer coming from her friend.

Mara pushed the speed limit to the maximum and they were in Springfield in 20 minutes. A State Trooper was waiting on the outskirts of town, and Mara pulled into the Walgreen's parking lot where he told Heather he'd be waiting.

"I am Officer Ballard. The commander asked me to come over and meet you. He can't leave the site right now. Please follow, and stay close behind me, we'll need to negotiate traffic and at some point, you'll park your car and ride the rest of the way with me."

Heather was trembling as she got back into the car. She didn't have to ask if one of the officers was Joe, she could tell by looking at his face. Was he wounded or dead? She started praying again for both of the Troopers.

They drove in silence behind the patrol car with lights flashing and siren sounding. Mara's heart was pounding so hard she thought it was going to come through her chest. She couldn't imagine what Heather was feeling right now.

The patrol car swung into a parking lot and got out of his car. "You'll need to go the rest of the way with me. Don't worry, we'll look after your car, nothing will happen to it while you're gone."

They hurried to the officer's car, Heather was shivering, and the officer turned on the heater and directed it toward her. "Mrs. Davis, we aren't certain but we are sure that your husband and another officer in the area, Mark Hunter were the first responders to the call. After that, it's murky about how it went down. We have various eyewitness accounts and we are still trying to get close enough to get to our officers. Every time we make a move toward them, the shooter starts firing at us. He's released two of his hostages, but he's threatening to kill his ex-wife and himself. We're using negotiators now trying to resolve the situation. He's using his wife's cell phone, we have the number, and we're trying to talk him into surrendering. Or at least letting us go get our men."

"Oh," Heather's voice was barely a whisper.

Soon, they came to police barriers, allowed through by another officer, they drove through. Mara recognized the building she couldn't believe it had been less than a week since she had been in this spot. It looked different now. TV crews with their vans and cameras were everywhere. Police and state patrol cars blocked the street off in front of the building.

"Follow me," said Jack. He pushed his way into the crowd, pushing aside microphones and scowling at reporters that tried to crowd him. They stopped behind an armored van. Officer Booth walked over to another officer to confer with him about any updates since he had left the scene. Mara put her arms around Heather, took off her own jacket to put around Heather's shoulders. Her friend was shaking hard enough her teeth chattered

Officer Booth came back. There aren't any new developments. Our SWAT team is in place and we're only waiting on the Commissioner to give us the word. We don't want any more casualties, but we need to get to our officers too. This has been going on for over three hours. My Officers need medical attention and I'm not willing to allow this crisis to go on much longer. He's demanding to see his three young children and we don't believe it would be in anyone's best interest to do that."

The ringing of his cell phone interrupted him. Answering, he walked a short distance away. They could only hear muffled words, but his face showed worry lines as he walked back over to them. The commissioner has called to give permission to go after the hostage taker. We'll try to talk to him one more time, then we're going in after him."

They watched as the negotiator made a last desperate try to talk the man into surrendering. The gestures and his facial expressions told them he wasn't making any headway with him.

"We can't wait any longer, if our men are going to have a chance at all, we have to get them out of there NOW!" The gunmen fired another shot from behind a column aiming at the squad cars.

Jack Ballard gave the order. "Go get him." The SWAT team sprang into action. With covering fire from across the street, the team stormed up the Capitol stairs. They knew more were slipping in behind the man. Two shots rang out, and Heather screamed. The SWAT team continued their assault moving up the steps getting closer and closer. No more shots rang out, they cautiously moved in closer.

"Get some EMT's here now. The man is dead and his wife is in bad shape. Get our men out now."

The officers went into action, the paramedics running first to the squad cars and others up the steps to take care of the woman. Medical equipment came out of bags, and there was a call for stretchers.

"I'm going to go up there now," he told Heather. "Please you and your friend stay here until I come back and give you word."

They stood in mute silence, with the cacophony of sound all around them; they wouldn't

be able to hear each other anyway. Heather was still shivering and Mara still had her arms around her, trying to give as much comfort as she could.

Officer Ballard come running back to them. "Get in the car; both officers are going to St. John's Hospital. I'll drive you, one of them is Joe, and he's alive, hang on to that hope."

Chapter 25

Sirens were blaring as they followed the two ambulances to the hospital. Heather asked, "Who was the other officer?"

"The other officer is Mark Hunter, his wife is on her way right now. It took us a while to find her, she was visiting her Mother in Decatur. Her brother is driving her over and her Mother is staying with her baby."

"Oh, I know Mark and Tina, what a nice couple and their baby is only a few months old. I hope he'll be all right. Joe and I went to see her and the baby at the hospital. He was so excited. Thirty years old and finally he has a new daughter, he felt his life was complete. He finally had a family of his own. We invited him over for dinner before they met, and he adored JJ, and was in total awe of Melody. It's going to be horrible for Tina."

Mara marveled that her friend could think of someone else, not knowing if her husband would be all right or not. She understood now, she had a friend in a million. One who thought of other people before she worried about her own troubles. Tears sprang to her eyes; she was so lucky to have a friend like Heather. She silently prayed for the two wounded men.

Pulling up to the emergency entrance, hospital staff rushed out to maneuver the stretchers into the emergency room. One set took Mark, the other set grabbed Joe's stretcher. Heather started to follow, but one of the nurses gently took her by the arm and told her she would need to wait in the waiting room. She'd only be in the way and they were doing all they could do to save her husbands life. Heather shook her head and sat down in a chair. It was as if her legs had turned to jell-o and couldn't support her any more. The nurse saw that she was going to stay put and hurried off to join the rest of the staff working to save Joe's life. The TV in the corner of the waiting room was blaring, it was Friday night and the sitcoms were on. Mara quickly went to turn it off, there wasn't anyone else in the waiting room, and the canned laughter was grating on her nerves.

They didn't have to speak; they waited and prayed for Joe and Mark. Tina came into the room, dazed and in shock. The Trooper stepped away and Heather rushed over to hug her and try to console her. Choking up, they started talking, each of them worried about their husbands.

A nurse came in and looked at both wives, "Both of these men have lost a tremendous amount of blood. A call has already gone out to their co-workers for them to come in and donate blood. Mrs. Hunter, Mark is in a coma that's we've medically induced because of the trauma to his body where he took the bullet. It came close to his spinal column and we need to keep him stabilized until he's able to have surgery to have it removed. One movement the wrong way could paralyze him. We don't want that to happen."

She turned to Heather, "Mrs. Davis, your husband is not as seriously wounded as Officer Hunter. He has lost however, a great deal of blood. The bullet missed all of his major organs but we need to get his blood level up. I think he'll be all right."

" When can we see them?" Asked Heather.

"Let us get them stable and cleaned up. After they've had a transfusion, we'll see how they are. They'll be going to Intensive Care and visits have to be short and limited strictly to immediate family of course, five minutes every two hours. Meanwhile, is there anything we can get for you? We have a Priest and a Minister here always, I would be glad to send one of them up for you both. There is coffee in the little room right over there, as well as a rest room. There are soft drinks and juice in the refrigerator. Here's a phone you can use to call your families. Please feel free to come to the nurse's station anytime and we'll give you an update on their status. We won't be upset and it won't bother us, we're concerned about both you and your husbands right now." With that, she turned and left the room.

Tina's brother, Tim entered the room and they filled him in on what was happening. They sat in silence. The inactivity finally getting to him, Tina's brother suggested that he go back to Decatur and take care of his niece allowing their Mother to come to the hospital. He kissed her good-bye and nodded to Heather and Mara, "You know they'll both be in my prayers, I love you Sis."

The silence was overwhelming, all they could hear were the voices of the staff going up and down the hallway. Officer Ballard came in, "You should see the hall downstairs lined with troopers standing in line ready to give blood. It makes me proud to be part of such a great team. Is there anything I can do for you ladies? I'll be glad to go down to get you a sandwich, or a cup of coffee."

They all declined, no one felt hungry, and they were waiting on a nurse or Doctor to give them the latest word on the two men. The clock seemed to tick slowly, to Mara it felt every time she checked it, five minutes was all that passed.

A nurse entered the room with a smile on her face, "Mrs. Davis, you may visit your husband for five minutes, he's awake and asking for you."

Heather jumped up and followed the nurse out of the room.

Mara went over to sit next to Tina. "I'm Mara, Heather's friend, may I sit here with you till your Mother comes?"

Tina nodded her head and extended her hand. Mara held her hand, stroking and patting just as she had seen Heather do for Melody to calm her down. Officer Ballard walked in with a tray of four hot coffees. Coffee, cream sugar and vending machine cookies filled the tray.

"I thought someone might want something to nibble on, and I figured coffee couldn't hurt, it's going to be a long night. The wife of the shooter went to the other hospital and we've just received word that she didn't make it. So sad, and so useless, now there are three children who will grow up without their Mother or their Father."

Heather came back in, looking white and shaken. "He has tubes all around him, but he's awake and he knew I was there. He tried to talk, but he's just too weak. I assured him that Mara was here with me, and then he dropped off to sleep again."

She sagged into the nearest chair. "I think he'll be all right." Then she burst into tears.

Emotion and tension thick and heavy as a wool blanket filled the room.

Tina looked up as a Doctor walked in to the room. "Mrs. Hunter, your husband is now stable. We've given him blood but he is still however in an induced coma. We want him to stay as still as possible until we think he's ready for surgery to get that bullet out of him. Come with me, I'll take you to him."

Tina stood up and followed him out of the room. They watched her, walking away on shaky legs. Officer Ballard jumped up, took her by the arm, and walked with her down the hall.

Chapter 26

The hours crawled by. Tina's Mother arrived and reassured Tina. Tim and his wife were caring for her baby. They were parents of a 2-year old, and had everything that they would need for five-month-old Katlin. Every two hours, a nurse came in and took each wife to see her husband. The nursing staff alternated between Tina and Heather so one of them was gone for five minutes. Officer Ballard left, but another State Trooper came to take his place. They curled up in chairs and tried to sleep, the nurses brought them blankets and pillows. Everyone was trying to make it as easy on the women as possible.

Mara thought, Tina and Heather have a true marriage. I didn't know it could be like this. Isn't that amazing? I'm 26 years old and didn't know two people could be so close. There is such an emotion as love. I know it now, just by watching how Tina and Heather handle their emotions and the love they are displaying. To Mara, this was new vision of how life can be if two people loved each other. She suddenly hoped that she would find that someday. She was lonely and just now figuring it out. A successful career, good job, nice apartment, and a pet would never replace what she now wanted so desperately. I want love, I deserve to it. With that thought, she drifted into a troubled sleep. The dream came back. It was the same dream and it didn't give her any more insight this time. She woke up shivering. I will know, I will learn the truth and make a different life for me. She slept dreamless for another few hours.

The dawn brought more activity and hope for both women. The nursing staff moved Joe into a private room, Mark was stable, and the Doctors were planning on performing surgery today. The women hugged one another and rejoiced at the good news.

"Tina, I'll be here at the hospital, I won't leave Joe, in case you need me. I'll sit with you while Mark is in the operating room, we'll get through this, together. Mara, you need to go home and settle into your apartment. You'll be starting work on Monday; you can't be exhausted on your first day. I'll be fine now, and I know that Mother is with the kids. If you would check in with her and give her the news, I would appreciate it. Thanks for being here for me, I don't know what I would've done without you." She gave Mara a hug, turned, and went down the hall to Joe's room.

"Tina, I'll be praying for you and your husband. I'll come back tonight. I intend to bring Heather a change of clothes and some personal items. Can I bring anything for you?"

"Thanks, but no, my Mom brought me a suitcase when she came and I'm going to clean up and change clothes before they take Mark to surgery."

"All right, I'll see you later. I know everything will be fine."

Mara walked out of the hospital and looked up at the clear autumn sky. I know it's going to be all right, Tina and Mark, Heather and Joe, and I'll be fine too.

The ride home was uneventful; she popped in another favorite CD. She listened to Toby Keith, singing upbeat tunes to help her stay awake. She decided she would go to Heather's, relay the message Heather had sent her and then go to her own apartment. She had a few housekeeping chores she wanted to do, but knew she would be comfortable. She wanted to take a nap so she'd be alert enough to drive back to Springfield tonight.

In Illiopolis, she found everything running as usual at Heather's home. Heather's Mom was busy in the kitchen doing dishes, JJ was watching Saturday morning cartoons, and Melody was in her high chair playing and jabbering at her Grandma. Mara related everything that was happening, eased her mind about Joe, and promised to stop by late that afternoon to pick up a small suitcase of essentials to take back. She thought about going by her Mother's shop to fill her in, but decided to call her instead. She needed to get some rest and do a little grocery shopping.

She dialed her mom's salon phone, "Mother, I just called to let you know that Heather's husband Joe is going to be all right. He is stable and is out of ICU and in his own room. I've been with her since I left your house and I need to go to my apartment, get some rest and run some errands. Thanks for dinner last night, I hope to see you again soon." She knew her Mother had a customer and could only talk for a minute or two, she felt hurt when her call only lasted a few minutes, and a visit left hanging in the air.

Pulling into her parking spot in the garage, Mara walked up the stairs to her apartment. She unlocked the door and went in. She felt at home here, and was happy she could fall into an already made bed. She set her alarm for three o'clock and after taking a quick shower, went to bed. This time her sleep was dreamless and untroubled.

When the alarm went off, she felt refreshed and ready to tackle whatever else might come today.

She felt a new sense of purpose, a new reason for living. She could look toward the future with confidence. She knew she was a different person then the scared teenager who fled her hometown that night more than eight years ago. She was stronger; she'd be able to deal with her parents, and the secrets her past might hold.

Dressing casually in jeans and a sweatshirt, she drove over to the grocery store to pick up a few groceries. She needed some soda, and something for lunch. She lived close enough to her work; she could come home for lunch and relax on her lunch hour. She'd noticed a pet store at the shopping center and decided she would go in there the first chance she got and find her a kitten. She also intended to sign up at the tanning salon; she felt the effects of shorter days, and lack of sunshine.

Returning home, she put her groceries away and prepared to drive back to Springfield. She would stop in Illiopolis and pick up the suitcase that would be ready for Heather, and then she would go see how the two women were holding up. She hoped the surgery had gone well for Mark and was anxious to hear he was out of danger.

Heather's Mom met her at the door. "Hi Mara, come on in, I have a suitcase for Heather and the children made their Daddy a card to send to him. I am sending some chocolate chip cookies I baked this afternoon over to them and some for Tina and Mark too. Of course, there is a package to take to your new apartment. I had a call for you today, someone named Jerry Lowe. He left his phone number and asked that you give him a call sometime."

Mara took the cookies and the phone number. She would call him, but she knew she had a long way to go before she'd be ready for a relationship with him or any man. She had too much to learn, too much growing to do. She wasn't ready yet for a man to complicate her life. She went in to kiss JJ and Melody, they shrieked and ran to her with their arms held open. Their little bodies fragrant from a recent bath, they felt good to hold. She felt her heart opening wider in response to their little hugs. She felt happy and content right now. She wanted nothing to disturb the peace she was feeling at this moment in her life. She quieted the voice that told her, you know you're just waiting for the other shoe to drop. Life can't go this smoothly, it isn't natural. Just wait, when something happens it'll knock you for a loop. She shook her head, that was her old self-talking. She let her mind wander to her secret place. Sitting by the ocean, looking at the blue sky and the sun warm on her face, she started thinking positive thoughts, pushing the old voice out of her head.

Chapter 27

Mara arrived at the hospital and went first to Joe's room. She knew she could get the information on the other officer from Heather. It pleased her to see Joe with his bed up and trying to eat dinner. She dropped the suitcase by the bedside table and gave Heather a hug. I'm giving more hugs in just this last week, then in my whole lifetime.

"Mara, thanks for bringing me some clean clothes and deodorant. I can use a shower, and staff told me I could use the one here in Joe's room. This chair turns into a twin-size bed, so I'll be staying here at least for one more night."

"How is Mark? Did his surgery go all right? How's Tina holding up? She's been in my thoughts all day."

"Mark's surgery was long, but it was successful too. He's still in a coma, but they're going to start letting him wake up tomorrow. They want to make sure that he has feeling in his arms and legs, but felt he needed to rest a little longer. Tina is in the waiting room if you'd like to go see her."

"Your Mother sent some cookies for you and Joe, also for Tina and Mark. I'll just step down the hall and deliver them to her. I want her to know that I've been praying for Mark today, and I'm happy the surgery went so well."

Mara walked down to the ICU waiting room, finding Tina stretched out on the couch. Her brother was there also; watching the news on TV.

"Tina, I just wanted to tell you how happy I am that Mark's surgery was successful. I am sure there will be a long recovery time, but I'm glad that he'll make it."

Tina looked like she was feeling better but Mara could tell the long night and day had taken a toll on her.

"Here's some cookies that Heather's Mom made, she wanted to make sure you got some too."

"Oh, isn't she sweet? People have been so good to help me out with whatever I need. Officer Booth was in for most of the day, sitting with me while Mark had surgery. Thanks to all the State Troopers, Mark had enough blood when he needed it in surgery. Its times like this, you find out who your true friends are. I'm glad I can count you as one."

Mara blushed at the offer of friendship with a woman who had just gone through so much. She would treasure their friendship and she told Tina so. She walked back down the hall to Joe's room. He was quietly resting after finishing his dinner.

Heather whispered, "The Doctor thinks he'll be able to go home by Wednesday. Isn't that wonderful? I have so much to be thankful for."

Mara nodded her head. It seemed like this one week had lasted forever because of what had happened. She talked to Heather a little about her job, and the progress she was making on her apartment. She also offered to go down to the sandwich shop and bring her up something to eat. Heather declined stating the nurses had made sure she had been able to get a dinner tray also.

"Heather, your Mom has everything under control, and I think she's working on Halloween costumes. I didn't realize Halloween was tomorrow."

"Oh good, that is one less worry on my mind. I plan to stay here tonight then going home tomorrow afternoon, so I can take the kids trick or treating. I'll have to take pictures and bring them here for Joe to see."

" I know they'll be so adorable," said Mara. "I'll run out there tomorrow with some special treats for them. I don't know how many children are in my neighborhood, so I'm leaving the light out this year so they won't come to the door. I have plenty to do before I start work on Monday."

"Mara, I just want to thank you for all you've done for me. I know God sent you back to Illinois at the right moment. You are a Godsend. If there is anything I can ever do for you, please let me know. I have a lot to repay you for."

"Heather, between friends there are no scorecards. You helped me when I came back, now I'm helping you. Friends do that, there's nothing to repay."

The eight years that passed between the last times they met, until this moment, didn't matter one bit. The two women were as close as sisters were and the tragedy of what just happened brought them even closer. Mara felt so fortunate that she came back to Illinois, not only for her own peace of mind, but because Heather would need her also. She didn't believe anything happened by accident, there was a master plan behind it all. They just might not see the whole picture for a longtime.

Joe was sleeping peacefully and the two friends sat quietly and chatted. Mara told her a little more about what her job would involve and shared how excited she was to have found it. Heather asked if her kids looked like they were doing ok.

"I think the kids are just fine. They have their Grandma wrapped around their little fingers, and I bet they're having the time of their lives. Who wouldn't have fun making cookies with Grandma and playing dress up with Halloween costumes that Grandma made?"

"You're so right; my Mom will spoil them rotten before I get home." They laughed; it was good to feel tension free for a time.

Joe woke just then, "What's so funny?"

Heather explained what JJ and Melody had been up to since she had been at the hospital with him. He smiled and agreed with them, he knew how much they loved their Grandma.

Mara stood up, "I'm going to go home now, and leave you two some private time. I may not be back tomorrow, but I'll be going to Illiopolis to see the kids dressed up in their costumes and taking them some goodies. Then Monday is my first day at the new job. I want to focus on my job so I can give it my best"

"Goodnight Mara, thanks for being with my wife during this ordeal. We'll never forget what you've done for us," said Joe.

Heather stood up to walk her to the elevator. They stopped by the ICU waiting room, but it must have been time for Tina's visit and they missed her.

"I'll tell her you stopped by again, she'll appreciate it. Night Mara, be careful going home and again, thanks for everything. You've been terrific, I love you!"

"It was nothing that anyone else wouldn't have done, but I recognize the emotion behind the thank you. You and Joe, and of course JJ and Melody have become like my family in a short time. I'm so glad I was here to be with you." Heather gave Mara a huge hug and Mara found it easier than ever to accept one from her best friend. It's getting easier, I am getting stronger, and I'm feeling more emotions.

The ride home took the usual amount of time, but instead of listening to her CD's, she thought about the last few days. Yes, she knew there was a change within her. She tried to pinpoint when she first felt herself let go. Accepting friendship, help and hugs were new to her. She felt she had come a long way. She thought about her new job on Monday, and knew she would enjoy it. Yes, my life is looking brighter all the time.

She whispered a prayer of thanks and sent it heavenward so God wouldn't think she was ungrateful.

She thought about the phone number she clutched as she left Heather's house today. Mara felt flattered and amazed that someone was expressing an interest in her. She knew she would have to call and explain the situation to Jerry. He wouldn't understand, but she had to take care of her own issues first. She needed to understand her own life before getting involved with someone. She drove into the parking garage and realized how tiring the day had been. She would just go to bed tonight. She needed her energy for her new job on Monday.

She drank a glass of milk, and then soaked in a hot bubble bath. She was already starting to nod off before she got out of the tub. She turned down the bed, crawled in, and slept peacefully for the first time in a longtime.

Chapter 28

Mara woke feeling refreshed in her body and mind. She decided to feed her soul and prepared to attend the University Church. The Minister always posted the worship times on the sign out front. She would slip in quietly, listen to the sermon, and then come home. She was sure she wouldn't know anyone and was happy to listen to the traditional songs, and the peace that she knew it would give her. The changes she noticed in her life were amazing. She was happy to be starting to work on Monday and felt she would get along with her co-workers just fine.

The Church was beautiful, the music inspired her and she enjoyed singing a few of the hymns she used to sing as she was growing up. She left after the service feeling uplifted and revived. She hadn't seen anyone she recognized and decided to treat herself to a dinner at the local Mexican place.

She didn't mind sitting by herself in a restaurant. She had learned to do that when she was living alone in San Francisco. It could be tough to do, but when you feel your confidence level at an all-time high, it wasn't too bad at all. She enjoyed her meal and looked through the brochures she had picked up at the University. She wanted to know as much as possible about the school before she went to work there. She found that it was rich in history. Local families who believed in the University and wanted to see the private college succeed donated much of the money used for building and expanding. The pictures showed all the buildings were brick and fit in perfectly with the neighborhood. She read about the Fraternities and Sororities that had houses located there, and some of the many ways that Millikin participated in the community. Yes, this will be a good match for me, she thought.

She stuffed the brochures back into her purse and gave the server her Visa card. She marveled, I'm happy, how many times in my life have I been able to say that? The only thing I want to do now, is reconcile with my parents. She knew she'd tried to be the best daughter her parents could want, but always fall short in some way. After going through therapy, she could now see that it wasn't her fault. Her parents were not happy with their lives, and nothing she could do would make them happy. She felt inside that it had something to do with her, and she had to find the underlying cause of it, but for now, she would leave things alone. She needed to concentrate on her new job. She would keep in touch with her Mother, and if invited, would go again for dinner. Mara intended to take it slow and easy. She hoped she would have the patience to bide her time.

Going back to her apartment she finished arranging her few belongings. She would have time this week to do some errands and planned to pick up a few plants for her apartment. Joe was on the mend and Heather wouldn't need her as much as she had this weekend.

She had picked up a couple of Halloween bags and some treats when she went grocery shopping a few days ago. All she needed to do was to put her goodie bags together and take it out to Illiopolis. She couldn't wait to see the kids in their costumes. Driving out to Heather's home, there was a slight mist in the air. She hoped it would clear up for the children to go trick or treating without getting soaked. She could feel the nip in the air. It would be colder in the morning, she was sure. A deer running across the road startled her. She slowed down to a crawl. She knew one deer meant another one was nearby. She didn't want to be responsible for injuring or killing one, and she didn't want her car in the shop either. Sure enough, the other deer, a big buck soon came out of the field and ran right in front of her. She braked and stopped before she hit the beautiful deer.

Arriving at Heather's home, she found her best friend there. "Hi Heather, I'm glad you got to come home for a while. How's Joe? Have you talked to Tina to find out how Mark is doing?"

Heather smiled at Mara, "Do you know you sound like me now, firing question after question at me. I would've never dreamed you could be this outgoing. Joe is fine, he wanted me to come home and pick up a couple of books for him to read and get his shaving gear. That means he's feeling better and he's started bugging the nurses about coming home. Mark is doing better; he's awake and alert and has feeling in his arms and legs. They're moving him into a room tomorrow morning. He's still on IV's but he'll start rehabilitation soon. He'll need to keep his muscles moving so they don't contract on him. All in all, I think we both had our prayers answered when it comes to our husbands."

"Mommy, Mommy, look at me. I'm a clown and Melody is a princess. Grandma made our costumes, aren't we cute? JJ looked adorable with his clown suit, big shoes, long tie, and round red spots on his face. Melody came trailing after JJ. Mara thought she was the most beautiful little girl in the world. Dressed in a filmy long dress with a princess tiara on her head, she looked just like a little angel.

"Mama, I a princess!"

Heather scooped her up in her arms, and said, "Yes my little darling, you are a princess, and your Daddy wants to see a picture of you two. JJ come over here and stand with your sister so I can take your picture. Now smile, Daddy will want to see those happy faces!" With that, she snapped a couple of pictures with her digital camera.

"Now I can take this camera and show your Daddy how cute you two look."

Mara said, "JJ, Melody, here's a little goodie bag to put into your pumpkins. You will start trick or treating with something already in there."

The kids ran over to her and as she placed their bags into their pumpkins she gave them both a kiss. They were so excited, and JJ wanted to eat some of his candy right then. Their Mother quickly set him straight on that. "You will not have any candy until after you've had your dinner. Grandma will look through your candy to make sure there isn't anything in your goodies that would harm you. You can have some before you go to bed, but don't forget to brush your teeth when you're done eating candy."

Heather stood up. "I'm going back to the hospital for a while, but I'm coming home to sleep tonight. Joe's doing great and I feel the need for a good nights sleep in my own bed."

She went over to give her Mother a hug, "Thanks Mom for being here with the kids. I love you!" JJ and Melody, Mommy will be home tonight and I'll kiss you goodnight even if you're asleep. She gave them both kisses, hugs, and hurried out.

Then she hurried out the door. "Good luck tomorrow Mara, I'll be thinking of you, call me tomorrow night and tell me how it went."

"I need to go home as well, so you can take the kids trick or treating. Talk to you soon."

Chapter 29

Monday morning dawned crisp and cold with frost covering the car windows parked on the street. Mara was happy she had an enclosed parking spot so she wouldn't need to scrape her windows. She dressed with care in a gray pantsuit, cranberry top, and a pair of black stacked heels. They were stylish but comfortable; she didn't want her feet hurting her on her first day. She ate a banana and some toast, stocking up on energy. After straightening the kitchen she grabbed her purse and left for work. She wanted to be early so she could look through her office and stock up on supplies.

She felt her confidence rise as she was walking toward the administration building. I have a job I know I can do, and I'll enjoy it. I've gone from a quiet, shy, withdrawn little girl that could barely lift her eyes to someone talking to me, to a confident woman who likes to work with the public. That's a miracle.

Beth greeted her as she came in the door. "Good morning Mara, we're ready for you, I think we have everything you need in your office. Come and take a look."

Mara followed her down the hall to what had been an empty office. It was now a well-supplied office, ready for occupancy. She saw several plants sitting around the office. Looking at the cards, she noticed they came from several different departments at the University.

The computer was state of the art, and a new flat screen monitor set atop the desk.

"I'm overwhelmed," said Mara. "I can't believe how welcome everyone has made me feel."

"Carol will be in, but it's a little early for her yet. She'll come in around nine and work until six or so. I come in at seven and work until four, and Sam comes in at noon and goes home at five. Dean Hall is always around somewhere, but he spends time doing fund-raising events, and walking around the campus. He likes to keep in touch with the students. He's popular and has an open-door policy. He's available to students any time he's in the office."

Mara felt warmly welcomed, she belonged here and the welcome only confirmed that feeling.

"I'll let you settle in and let you look through the activities already planned. You have a meeting with Mia Fritz the alumni president at ten o'clock. Since you'll be working together she wants to meet you."

"I'll take you down the hall and show you where the break room and rest rooms are. There's always a pot of coffee on, and many times, there are cookies or doughnuts brought in by faculty or even students. I'm afraid they spoil us here. We love it."

Finally, Mara was alone in her office. She looked around and smiled, this was great. I know this position won't be without stress, but I'm going to love the challenge. She went to work, looking at the calendar of events the University had coming up. They were hosting the High School Turkey Tournament; they had several artists performing at the Fine Arts Center. There would be plenty to do to keep her busy. She noticed that some events had already passed. Homecoming, Parents weekend, and new student orientation all were over. She thought the basketball tournament would be her priority, and then the Vesper service and the Faculty tea. She scanned the copy of the local newspaper someone had left on her desk. She would need to get to know some of the reporters if she wanted good press coverage for events.

She called the newspaper office and introduced herself, asking to speak to the Editor. The secretary promised she would have him call back when he was available. He was chairing a staff meeting till noon. Mara wandered into the break room looking for a cup of coffee. She noticed a tray of doughnuts that hadn't been there earlier. She picked up her coffee and stayed away from the plate of temptation. She was always mindful that she used to be a fat teenager with acne all over her face. She had come too far to backslide into heaviness again.

Before she knew it, her 10 o'clock appointment was waiting for her. She told Beth she'd be right out. She walked down the hall and extended her hand to the woman who was standing in the reception area.

"Hi, you must be Mia Fritz, I am Mara Conley. It's good to meet you," she said smiling and holding out her hand.

"Yes, I'm Mia Fritz the Alumni Association President." She held out her hand but her handshake was a bare touch of the fingers. Her business suit and her upswept hairstyle, in fashion from head to toe made her look intimidating. "I hope we'll work well together."

She turned and swept down the hallway, turning into Mara's office. "Well, let's see what you can do."

Mara followed and sat down at her desk. This isn't going to be easy. She must think I'm taking some of her authority from her. Mara said, "I'm looking forward to getting to know you and hope we will be able to help each other."

Mia sniffed and put her nose in the air. "I wasn't aware they were going to hire another person for this job. The last person didn't last six months. I don't understand why there's such a turnover with this position."

Mara thought, Well, I can guess what part of the problem is. I will not let her ruin this job for me; I'm not the dumpy little shy girl I used to be. I can hold my own against the best of them.

Mara smiled, "Tell me what you have planned so far, and we will go from there. I'm sure you have things well in hand for the next few events. Let's go over the plans and I'll see if there's anything I can add to them."

Their meeting lasted for an hour and a half. Exhausted Mara thought, She's going to be my thorn in the flesh, she thought. I am strong, and I will win her over or she'll try to get me fired. I can handle this; I've been in this position before. There's always one in every crowd. You've met her and you'll tackle her issues head on.

She decided to drive home for lunch and get away from the campus for an hour. It only took five minutes to get from the administration building to her apartment door. She took a moment to call Heather's to make sure things were still going well, then she decided to call her Mother at home. This was Monday; her Mother never opened the shop on Sunday or Monday.

"Mother, how are you? Yes, it's been busy and I've been helping Heather out with Joe in the hospital. Yes, I started my new job today and I love it. How's Father? Did it upset him too much the other night? I would love to come by this weekend to see you both again. Can I bring something over for dinner? I could stop and get take out here in Decatur before I drive out."

Mara listened to her Mother's comments, she was agreeing for Mara to come out again on Friday night. She wanted to fix dinner because her husband was particular about his food and hated eating food wasn't homemade. I should have remembered that. Oh well, at least I can go see them, maybe I will learn a little more this time. She knew she was going to ask about the genetic eye disease. She wanted to find out something before she made her appointment with the specialist in Springfield.

She fixed a small lunch and sat in front of the TV. She caught up on the world news on the FOX news channel. She was feeling a little stressed, a combination of the meeting with Mia that morning, and the conversation with her Mother. She clicked off the TV, leaned back, and closed her eyes. She practiced deep breathing and used her favorite visual meditation tool. She was at the beach, the sun was warming her skin, and the breeze was blowing lightly through her hair. She didn't have a care in the world; the beach was empty except for her. She could hear the seagulls, and the gentle lapping of the waves as they crept up to the shore. She was looking for her inner peace. As it had worked in the past, it worked now and she felt ready to go back to finish the day.

The rest of the day went well, with Dean Hall came in to welcome her to the staff and tell her that if there was anything she wanted, to come to him. She met Sam, who looked barely 15, but was 25 with an infant at home. She was funny, chatty, and had a smile on her face. Mara liked her already. She would at least have a personal assistant who was positive and upbeat. That would be a big plus for her. Sam had long blonde hair, bright blue eyes, and the whitest teeth Mara had ever seen. She soon found out that Sam's father was a dentist, which was her secret to such great teeth. She looked at pictures of Sam's new daughter Kelli and learned her husband worked as a lineman for the local power company. This little part of her world would be just fine.

She looked at the clock and wondered where the hours had gone. She felt as if she had just gotten to work and it was time to go home. She said goodnight to Sam who was also getting ready to leave, stopped in to say goodnight to Carol and walked to her car. She left the office tired but happy. She noticed a few days before there was a Wing Stop restaurant down at the shopping center. That sounded good to her and would be easy and she would have a salad with it.

She drove down to the shopping center, while circling to find a parking place, she noticed the pet store was still open. Impulsively she decided to go in and look. The puppies captivated her, but she knew she wouldn't have time to care for a dog. She wandered over to the cat cages. They were all so cute, but wait, there was one little one in the back of one cage. It was smaller than the rest of the litter. Mara looked at her; the kitty didn't even come to the front of the cage as the rest of her siblings did.

She just looked at Mara as if to say, well I know you won't want me either. One of her ears looked a little chewed, and she was scrawny. She did have beautiful colorings. She looked like she had a target painted on her side. She had long fur that looked like it needed brushed. You look so neglected. I know how you feel, I've felt that way before too. You can come home with me and we will love each other.

The clerk tried to discourage her from taking the runt, but Mara was determined it was the kitten she wanted. She asked her to round up all the supplies she would need and told her she would be back to get everything after she picked up her dinner. She walked down to the take out place, placed her order, and took it back to the car. Then she went in to pick up her new kitten. Poor baby, she was cowering on the counter with a new collar around her neck. She looked so forlorn and lost. Yep, you're the right pet for me. We will get along great. She took out her Visa card, paid for her purchases, picked up the kitten, and walked out to her car. The poor thing was shivering; Mara put her under her jacket and zipped it up. She could feel her nestling in and slowly the shaking was gone. To Mara, it was one of the highlights of her day.

She ate her dinner; played with her kitten, showed her the apartment and where the litter box would be and then she then found herself dozing in the chair. It had been a long day with many emotions; she was too tired to stay awake to watch the evening news. She curled up in bed and soon felt her kitten jump up on the bed. She still didn't have a name yet;

she'd have to think about it before she made up her mind. Soon she was asleep, the kitten purring right beside her.

Chapter 30

The rest of the week went by in a blur. The days were constantly busy at the office. She loved the diversity of the job, and she adored the people she worked with. They were friendly, helpful and encouraging, well most of them anyway. She continued to have problems with Mia Fritz. Mara hoped that time and patience would win her over. She had one of the worst co-workers in history at one of her temporary jobs in San Francisco, but had eventually won her over by killing her with kindness. She felt sure she could work the same magic here.

During the week, she met regularly with Dean Hall, Carol, and Mia Fritz. Only small amounts of planning of the events coming were completed. The Editor of the newspaper called her back and she arranged to meet with him in his office. She wanted to get off on the right foot with him; she would need all the goodwill from the press she could get. She knew from experience it was important to network, for the good of the University. She would begin with him.

Several faculty members popped in during that first week, just to welcome and offer their support to her. Mara felt fortunate to work with such a wonderful group of people. She also called Heather several times to check on Joe. He had come home on Wednesday and would be recuperating for at least a month. His supervisor wanted him healed, and he would be getting some counseling for emotional healing as well. She told Heather she would stop by on Friday night after her dinner with her parents. She wanted to talk over the week with her friend, see if she could come up with any more suggestions on how to deal with Mia.

Most evenings, she went home immediately after work, had dinner, played with the kitten, and went to bed. She felt drained, and knew it would take a while to get into the routine of working every day again. Mara was happy; she loved what she was doing. She enjoyed the interaction with the students, she made it a point to come out of her office and introduce herself when she heard students in the outer office. She was thankful everyday she could look forward to going to her job. She knew there were some people that couldn't say that.

Often she took papers across the street to the Alumni administration building. She always made a point to speak to Mia, compliment her on her outfit and always smiled warmly at her. Somehow, someway, Mara wanted to make this woman a friend. On one of her trips, she walked around the front of the campus, admiring the structure, and the color of the leaves. It was a gorgeous time of year. She also had gone over to the Athletic Center and signed up for membership. During the winter, she would go over there, work out, and walk around the track to get her exercise. She hadn't strayed too far from the West end yet. Heather had promised to take her downtown to visit some of the shops on Merchant Street but that wouldn't be for a while yet. She had to take care of Joe; he needed much tender loving care right now.

She also knew that Mark was struggling to regain the use of one his legs. The muscles had started to contract on him and a sling was recommended for a short time to keep his leg straight. Both men wanted badly to get back to their work.

Illiopolis had rallied around Heather's family, bringing in food, taking the children for a few hours to give their Mother a rest and even cleaning house for her. She started helping in JJ's school again, but not as often as she did before the shooting. Mara knew her friend wouldn't be able to stay away too long, but Joe was independent. He would soon be insisting that Heather leave and give him some breathing room.

It was Friday before she knew it. The day was hectic but Mara enjoyed every moment of it. She went home to her kitty, and prepared to go to her parent's house. She was a little apprehensive about the visit. For some reason it made her uneasy, she didn't know why. She took several deep breaths and made her shoulders relax. You are not the same person you were when you left. You need answers and you are within your right to ask questions, she thought. Quickly changing her clothes she put on jeans and her favorite Old Navy sweatshirt. It was colder outside and rain was falling, she knew her parents would have the thermostat down low regardless of the weather. Ok, let's roll.

The drive was quiet and uneventful, she kept a close eye out for deer, they were especially bad this time of year, and she didn't want to hit one. She remembered Joe's story about the deer and had to laugh. Joe was an entertaining guy, he had a dry humor that you had to listen close to catch, but it was there. She was so happy that he was going to be all right. She drove on, only about 20 minutes to get to Illiopolis from where she lived. She had her favorite CD in and sang with Tim McGraw. We carry on, when our lives come undone. That's my motto, she thought.

She got out of the car pulling her jacket around her. The wind seemed a little more blustery here than it did in Decatur. The door opened as she was walking up; the steps.

"Hi Mother. I'm glad to see you."

Her Mother had a worried frown on her face. "Your father hasn't been having a good day today. He's mumbling all the time, agitated and sometimes he's getting a couple of coherent words out. I think he's just too agitated for visitors Mara."

Mara looked at her Mother, she saw the strain in her eyes, but she replied. "I'm already here now, so I'm staying. Maybe I can help with him."

"I doubt it, but come on in. I think your visit will just upset him more."

Mara followed her Mother to the kitchen instead of going to the living room to say hello to her Father. "What's wrong with him?"

"I don't know, but he's been upset all day. Bob came over this afternoon and I had to cancel a couple of appointments so I could come home to be with him. Bob just said he had been talking about how good it was to see you, and how nice you looked. John started in with his talking about then, and he was getting worse, so Bob called me home."

Mara picked up the plates and silverware, laying them out on the dining room table. From there, she could hear her Father mumbling, and sometimes a word was coming out almost in a shout. Now she knew why she felt so uneasy. This wasn't going to be an easy night.

Going back into the kitchen she asked, "Is there anything else I can do to help?"

No thank you, I have it all ready to set on the table. Since I came home early I had plenty of time to fix his favorite dinner and even baked a cherry pie."

"Mmmmm sounds good."

"I'll go get your Father, you go ahead and sit down."

Mara went to the dining room. She could hear murmurings coming from the living room, and the sound of the local news silenced. She was uneasy. There was so much tension in the house tonight.

Chapter 31

Her Mother rolled the wheelchair in and placed John at the head of the table. It was his usual spot. He looked at Mara, words forming on his lips, but no sound was coming out.

"Mara, its best if we just talk between us and try to ignore him. He sometimes will calm down that way."

They began talking in-between bites. Mara told her Mother about her job, and how much she enjoyed it. The baked chicken was delicious, and she loved her Mom's mashed potatoes and gravy. They also had green beans, another one of Mara's favorites and hot rolls.

"I had Lana bake those hot rolls especially for tonight. I remember how much you love them."

A sound came from her Father, she looked over at him. He was staring at her, trying to form words.

"What Father? What are you trying to say?"

He waved his good hand at her, as if saying, 'be quiet' I have something to say. He was struggling hard to get some words out. She sat there patiently; her Mother had gone still, waiting to know what he would try to say. She was pale and trembling.

"Mmmarra"

That single word shocked both women. Thrilled to hear her name come from his lips, she started to answer back. He interrupted her, with words barely legible she heard him say, "No daughter."

"What does he mean Mother?" She began to feel panic rising in her chest.

John was struggling and again he spoke, mumbled and barely understandable but the words were unmistakable that were coming out of his mouth.

"Not my daughter."

Her Mother gasped and put her hand on his arm. "John, please, this isn't the time. Please John, let me take you to your room."

"Nooooooo." That word was plain as day. He fidgeted in his chair, trying to get more words out. He looked at her, and she thought I have never seen love come from those eyes. He barely looked at me when I was growing up but now he's staring at me and trying to tell me something.

She looked over at her Mother. Tears had formed in her eyes and were dripping down her cheeks. "Please John, don't do this, and don't bring up the past. What's done is done."

Again, the long drawn out nooooo came out of his mouth. Struggling, he tried to form words; they could both tell that he was getting more and more agitated.

"John, please calm down. You're going to make yourself sick," said Mara's Mother.

Those words only made him worse. His color was bright red and his arms and legs were twitching.

"Hate you." Those words hung like a sword over the table. Mara was afraid to move. She was afraid of what she might hear next. Shocked and beyond speech, she could only stare at her Father.

Finding her voice she asked, "Mother, what does he mean?" Mara felt so lost and alone. She knew her Father hadn't wanted to be around her when she was little, but she didn't realize what he felt for her was hate. She wanted to believe that wasn't what he meant. She could remember making up happy stories to tell Heather about her Father sometimes, because she wanted to be normal, like everyone else. It had been a lie, what was going on?

"Father, what do you mean? What are you trying to say? Please tell me, I have a right to know." She had gone around the table to kneel beside his wheelchair. As she reached out to touch him, he shrank from her. She was stricken. She had loved this man as a Father all her life, even though she knew he didn't return her love. Now he was looking at her with hate filled eyes, and shrinking from her touch. Something was wrong here, something was very wrong.

Suddenly her Father went rigid. "Mother, call 9-1-1 right now; we need help here."

Her Mother ran for the phone while Mara stayed by her Father's side. She didn't dare touch him, he was so agitated already. Kneeling at his side, she talked to him, just meaningless talk, but she felt a need to fill the void. She talked to him about her job, her new apartment, and her best friend's family.

Barbara ran back into the room, "The emergency response team is on the way. They are close and should be here in a few minutes."

"Mother get a blanket to cover him with, he's shivering."

Barbara went to get a blanket and he looked at Mara, not with love, but his eyes said "Thank you."

Her mother's footsteps sounded on the stairs and she returned with a quilt she had made in the early part of their life together. This time, she could see the look of love in his eyes for his wife. *Why can't he look at me like that?*

The pounding on the door interrupted her thoughts. She ran to let the paramedics in. They pulled out their equipment and started an IV. Mara stood back as they put her Father on a stretcher and prepared to transport him to the hospital.

"Mother, you ride in the ambulance with him, and I'll follow in my car. Where will you take him?"

"His Doctor is in Decatur, we'll take him to Decatur Memorial Hospital." She climbed in after the stretcher to be with her husband on his way to the emergency room.

Mara pulled her car out of the driveway and followed the ambulance. She made a quick call to let Heather know what was happening. She was afraid, afraid she had caused this latest medical emergency. *No, you didn't make him upset, he was already upset when you came. You were only trying to be a daughter it isn't your fault. It isn't your fault; don't take the blame for this.* Mara kept the thought, repeating it over and over, it was her mantra.

Chapter 32

It seemed like hours before they reached the emergency room, even though she knew it was only about 15 minutes. She grabbed the first available parking spot and rushed to her Mother's side. The paramedics pulled him out of the ambulance and rushed him into the emergency room. While they took him away; Mara gave the information that they wanted. They told her his Doctor was on the way, and the emergency room doctor will attend to him until Dr. Finney got there.

Mara looked around impressed with the new emergency room. Each examining room had its own stool with a curtain around it, all necessary equipment and each had a TV mounted to the wall. Monitors hung from the ceiling keeping track of all the patients. Each room had sliding glass doors as well as a curtain to pull closed in front of them.

Her Father was lying still on the stretcher. No noise came from his mouth and his eyes, which looked so distant with her, but with so much love for her Mother, were closed.

The Doctor came in and asked them both to step out of the room. They stood outside his room and held hands. Mara's hands were as cold as her Mother's was. They were both shivering but with shock and not the cold. They were silent, both deep in their own thoughts.

The Doctor came out of the examination room; "We are taking Mr. Conley to have an MRI. The nurse will take you two ladies to the waiting area and I'll talk to you when we bring him back here. I want you to know we may need to admit him." They followed the nurse down the hall to the waiting room. It was nice and decorated to make everyone feel comfortable; but it was still a waiting room. A TV was on in the corner but no one was watching it. A sitcom with inane words coming from the actors mouths filled the screen. The words seemed inappropriate under the circumstances. A mother was waiting for her daughter, who had just had a miscarriage. She cried while she paced the floor while her daughter underwent a D and C.

Mara, thought, such a sad time for everyone. She offered a prayer for her Father and strength for her Mother. Then she said one for the unknown woman in the corner as well as her daughter. She was realizing what a real family could be. Yes, there are happy times, but sad times as well. Real families took care, supported one another, and most of all loved with all their hearts. She wished she'd known that sooner. It isn't too late. I can change the relationship between my Mom and me, even if it is too late for my Father.

"Mother, do you want me to get you a cup of coffee?" Mara asked.

"No thank you Mara, please just don't leave me right now." Mara took her hand and held on tight. She didn't know what to say, but if her presence was a comfort to her Mother then she'd stay by her side.

They waited quietly, neither one bringing up what had happened earlier. It wasn't the right time to talk about it. Lost in turmoil of thought; Mara didn't know what to think about what her Father had said at the dinner table. She had so many questions, but knew this wasn't the time to talk to her Mother about everything. A Doctor came in, but only to talk to the woman in the corner. Still they waited. It seemed like hours, but in reality had only been forty-five minutes.

The doors opened and the same nurse that had shown them into the waiting room was signaling them to follow her. They stood and walked behind her clutching hands.

She took them back to the emergency room where John had been when first admitted. The Doctor was standing by the bedside, and looked at them with sympathy in his eyes.

"I'm sorry to tell you Mrs. Conley that your husband has had another stroke. We didn't put him on a ventilator because we didn't know what your wishes would be. We can do that now, he's breathing on his own, but without the ventilator, he won't last long. We did an EEG and there is little or no activity, it will be just a matter of time. We are taking him to a room on the fourth floor. You will have more privacy there, and family will be able to contact you if they need to."

Barbara sagged; the nurse and Mara caught her and helped her to a chair. "He wouldn't want to live like a vegetable, I know he wouldn't. He's been so unhappy since he had his first stroke; he wanted to be active and busy."

Mara knelt beside her Mother. "This is a decision that you alone have to make. He's your husband and has been for nearly 40 years. I know it's difficult, but you have to do what you think he would want. Whatever you do, I'll support you in every way."

The Doctor said, "I'll leave you two alone for a couple of minutes, they'll be in to take Mr. Conley to his room. I will come up in a few moments and you give me your decision." The Doctor turned and left the room with the nurse following close behind.

"Mara, I know what I have to do. Living hooked up to a machine is not what he wanted. I love him, but I can't do that to him. What do you think?"

"Mother, I have been gone for eight years, you and Father love each other. You alone know what would be best for you and for him. I only ask that you give me a few moments alone with him before anything happens. I need to talk to him, even if he can't hear me or respond in any way. May I please?"

"Of course, you need that time, I understand that. We'll get him into a room and then I will go to the waiting room and let you spend time with him. When you're finished, come and get me and we will both stay with him."

Barbara left to tell the Doctor of her decision and the nurses came in to move her Father to a private room. They gave her a room number and directions to get through the hospital maze and wheeled him out of the room. Mara went in search of her Mother to take her upstairs. Her Mother told the Doctor of their decision. She wanted it to be different, but that was impossible.

They took the elevator up to the fourth floor to his room. The nurses asked that they stay outside until the nursing staff mad the transfer from the stretcher to the bed, and then they allowed them in.

"Mara, I will go down to the waiting room and give you private time with your Father. Please come and find me when you're finished and we'll stay here with him to the end."

She wished he could respond, but knew it was impossible. Where should she begin? She had so many emotions built up inside. Emotions she had tried to deny but were inside her and feelings that had to come out. She had no fear now. She knew he wouldn't look at her with distaste in his eyes, or shrink from her touch. She would tell him all she felt. It was time; she then could continue her own healing.

She took his hand in hers and began to tell him all she'd longed to tell him when she was growing up, before she went away, and since she had been home.

Chapter 33

"Father, no Daddy, I always wanted to call you Daddy. You insisted that I should call you Father and Mom, Mother, and I didn't understand that. I still don't understand why you had to be Mother and Father when other kids had Mommy's and

Daddy's. I felt it first when I went to kindergarten. Everyone else had his or her Daddy for a special Father's day play that night. Everyone, that is but me. I remember crying and Mother trying to console me, saying you worked hard all day and were tired. When we returned home, you were in the yard, working with your flowers. I didn't understand why you were too tired to come to my play, but you weren't too tired to work in the flower garden. Even then, you wouldn't give me a hug. I remember Mother telling me to give you a hug before I went to bed. I hugged you, but you never hugged me back.

I would hug you anyway, just because I loved the smell of the Old Spice you always wore. I can't smell Old Spice today without thinking of those good night hugs. It was the only time you ever let me touch you in any way.

I didn't understand, when I went to Junior High School, and you were so strict about me coming straight home from school. I didn't know why you would never allow a friend to spend the night with me, or why it was only a few times that you allowed me to sleep over with a friend. You didn't seem to care if I got a date for the Homecoming dance in High School, or the fact that I wasn't invited to Prom, not once in my four years of school. You didn't care if I was fat. You encouraged me by daring me to eat that second piece of pie, have a second or third helping of mashed potatoes or eat a bag of potato chips before I went to bed. I thought you were trying to help me by trying to shame me into losing weight. When I was an adult, I realized you weren't doing that. You were just being mean to me. Guess what Daddy? I loved you still. I would pretend you would come into my room to tuck me in, pray with me, and kiss and hug me goodnight.

I made excuses for you to my one best friend. I told her you were too tired to help me with my driving. I told everyone that I didn't want to go to the Father-Daughter banquet. That it would be a drag and no fun, but I cried that night in bed because I wanted to go so badly. All I ever wanted was your love. You gave me a home to live in, food to eat, and clothes to wear, but you would never give me your love. I didn't have one birthday party, and you never told me 'Happy Birthday'. Daddy, I don't know why, but I want you to know, I've always loved you. When I ran away, I imagined you were turning the world upside down to find me, but now I know you weren't doing that.

I still love you; I didn't mean to upset you further by coming home. I just wanted you and Mom to know that I turned out all right. I made something of myself, and I dieted and exercised and I no longer ate that second helping of mashed potatoes or a bag of chips before I went to sleep. I changed, grew up, and became more self-confident. I thought I had fallen in love with a man and I made the relationship work because it made me happy to have an older man interested in me. He treated me the same way you did when I was young, and I thought it was normal. After we broke up, it took three years of therapy to see I didn't know what a normal relationship was. I thought I was normal, and my best friend had the family that was strange. They enjoyed being with one another; they hugged and told everyone they loved them all the time. Did you ever say that to me Daddy? Did you ever, ever love me? I know there is a reason, but right now, I don't care. I have these words for you, I love you, and I always have and always will. I don't know why you couldn't love me back, but it doesn't matter any more. I know that I'll understand someday. Mother will talk to me now, and no matter what I find out, you're my Daddy I love you, and more important, I forgive you."

She stood up and gently kissed him on the cheek, put an arm around his lifeless body and gave him a hug, then went to get her Mom.

Mara walked her Mother back to the room where her Father lay. She stood outside the door so she would be near if her Mother wanted her. She could hear soft words and knew her Mother was crying. She didn't want to know what her Mother was saying to her husband. It wasn't her business to know. She had said all she needed to say and was at peace with her Dad. Yes, I can call you that now if I want. I can even call you Daddy. At least I've told you how much I loved you, and how badly you hurt me. I'll be fine now. Mother will tell me what I need to know and I can move on.

"Mara, please come in with me now. Sit down beside me. I need you near me. The Doctor told me when you were alone in here, that it shouldn't be too long. He will slip away peacefully and he's not in pain. We can be thankful for that."

They sat in silence, her Mother holding her Father's hand, and Mara holding her Mother's. A tear would slide down her Mother's cheek now and then. She told him repeatedly she loved him; stroking his arm and hand. Mara laid her head back on the chair and was not listening, but one phrase caught her attention. She thought she heard her Mother say talk to Mara tonight. She couldn't be sure, and right now, it didn't matter. The important thing now, was they were together as a family. Closer then they ever were. Ironic it had happened around her Father's deathbed.

The nurse slipped in to see if they were all right and quietly slipped out again. They were doing nothing for the man in the bed; their priority was for the two women who were sitting vigil watching over the man they both loved. She left behind two bottles of water and a couple of blankets to put around them. She understood it could be a long night.

The hospital grew quiet; visiting hours were over, but of course, they were exempt from that. They didn't leave his side through the long dark night. Now and then, someone would slip in the room, listen to the heartbeat, and feel the pulse of the dying man on the bed. Always, whoever came into the room would leave with a pat on the shoulder for both wife and daughter. The hospital chaplain came in and prayed with them, the word had gotten out. Barbara's pastor came during the night after hearing of what happened from Heather's Mom. Mara felt at peace with everything now. She knew her questions would be answered, she might not like what she heard, but at least she would know.

Mara laid her head back and dozed a small portion of the time, her Mother sat ramrod straight holding tightly to the man she had loved for over 40 years.

Mara stirred as her Mother gently touched her on the arm. "Mara, he's beginning to fail now. His breaths are shallow and are coming farther and farther apart. They listened and watched his chest move slowly in and out. There was a last gasp and he seemed to have a slight smile on his face. "He's gone now Mara. We need to say good-bye and let the Doctors and nurses do what they must do." She was quiet and in control, even though there was a slight quiver in her voice. They took one last look and walked out the door.

Chapter 34

Mara and her mother knew the man they loved had finally found peace and had gone to sleep and didn't wake up. No more frustration at not being able to perform everyday functions, or to communicate with his family or friends. They needed to make a few calls. The one to the funeral home in Illiopolis to arrange for burial was their first call. The funeral would take place in two days. They neither had any family left and since Mara was here, there was no reason to postpone the interment.

Mara used her cell phone to call Heather, and then to call her new boss. This was a bad way to start a new job, but she knew the administration would understand. Her job was not one of her worries, she knew she was the right fit for the position and so did her co-workers. She also made a call to Lana to let her know that her Father had passed away. She knew that her Mother wouldn't need to make a single call, the small town grapevine would go to work and when they got home, there would be phone messages from people saying they were bringing food. Lana would coordinate that effort and she had a key to the house, so no one would have to be home. Bob was right next-door, and he would keep an eye on the house.

"Mother, I need to go back to my apartment for a while. I will gather some clothes so I can stay with you for the next few days. I'm not sure what I'll do with my new kitten..."

"Bring her with you Mara, I always wanted a cat but your Father wouldn't hear of it, he thought the house would smell bad all the time. I would love to see her. May I even go with you? I don't want to be alone, although I know Lana would be over in a heartbeat"

Mara looked at her Mother, surprised. She was beginning to realize her Mother had been lonely too. She wondered what her parents lives had been before she entered their lives. Maybe someday, she would know. They thanked the nursing staff for being so kind to them and making them as comfortable as they could. The caring attitude of the whole staff had made the stay in the hospital easier for both of them.

They walked hand in hand into the bright sunlight. As they were walking through the doors, Church bells began to chime. They looked at each other and smiled. It was a fitting end to their night in the hospital.

"Do you need to go home before we go to Decatur?"

"No, I don't think I am ready for that yet. Lana went in last night, cleared the dining room table, and cleaned the kitchen. There's nothing for us to do there right now. Let's go to your apartment first, then we'll return home."

They rode in silence each deep in their own thoughts. They were each grieving in their own way. Mara had turned the CD off; Toby Keith's lighthearted tunes had no place in her car right now. There was a hint of frost on the barren cornfields. Soon it would be winter. Her heart felt frozen already.

When they reached Mara's apartment, she pulled into the garage and helped her Mother out of the car. She opened her apartment door and the kitten twined around Mara's legs.

"Oh Mara, she is so tiny, but so cute. What is her name?"

"To tell you the truth, I haven't had the time to give her a name yet. She has just been Kitty to me. I'll need to name her soon, I don't want to call her Kitty for the rest of her life."

Her Mother picked up the kitten, "Look, she has a target on her side, isn't that adorable, and look at this ear. Looks like a bigger kitten chewed on her a little, but she will gain weight now that she's in a loving home."

Mara looked at her Mother holding her first kitten. "I think I'll name her Hope. It seems fitting somehow, I have a new job, new future, and a new life with lots of hope. I think it's the perfect name for her."

"Hope, yes I can see why you would want to call her that. Well Hope, let's gather your food and litter box, and go visiting for a bit."

Mara was happy to see her Mother taking an interest in the kitten. She had unknowingly made the right move again. No, don't think that way. God has directed everything that's happened the last few weeks. Nothing happens by accident. She believed in divine direction.

She went to her room while her Mother roamed through the small apartment. "Mara this is such a cute apartment. If there is anything you need, I'm sure I have a spare of almost everything. Your Father would never throw anything away. I have items in the attic, I think you can use. I even still have some of your baby clothes. We can look up there when life has settled down some. My attic may surprise you."

The thought intrigued Mara, was there something in the attic that would help her understand? She knew she would need to bide her time. Rushing her Mother wasn't an option. Mara gathered her suitcase, the travel cage for Hope, litter box, and food to last for 3-4 days. "I think I'm ready to go, are you?"

Her Mother took a deep breath and shook her head yes. "I'm as ready as I'll ever be. The first time in the house will be the hardest, I'm so grateful you're here."

They rode back to Illiopolis in silence again. They didn't need any words between them. They now felt a new bond, a bond that had never been there when Mara was living at home. She marveled at the change. Maybe it was her; she knew she felt lighter and more peaceful after talking to her Father. Telling him everything she was feeling was a cleansing exercise. This was something her therapist had urged her to do for the last three years. Her Mother would also be under less stress, a little freer, a little more open. She was hopeful, yes, Hope was a good name for her kitten and for what she was feeling.

Chapter 35

They opened the door to the wonderful scent of cooking cinnamon rolls. Mara and her Mother spoke at the same time, "Lana is here."

Their neighbor came out of the kitchen with a flushed face and a look of concern. She went first to Barbara to hug her and then and hugged Mara. "I'm so sorry for your loss. I don't know what to say. Thank God in his mercy that he didn't suffer and was not in pain before he passed away. The two people that loved him surrounded him and we know he went to Heaven."

"The cinnamon rolls smell delicious. You know they've always been my comfort food. Thanks so much for making the house smell so wonderful and having them ready for us."

Lana just smiled. "Here is a list of those who have called and will bring food. I told them if no one was here, to bring the food to our house and we'll keep track of containers and names for you. I don't want you to worry about anything."

Mara gently took her Mother by the arm, "I think you rest for a bit. The next several days will be emotional and you haven't had any rest for two days."

"I am tired and think I could use a little nap," she replied.

Mara took her into the bedroom then drifted back to the kitchen. Lana had taken Hope from her cage, set up her bowl for water and food, and put the litter box just inside the door of the utility room.

A plate of cinnamon rolls, napkins and a tall glass of milk sat on the table. "I remember this was what you always wanted when you were sad or upset. Sit down honey, if you want to tell me about last night, it's ok. If you don't want to talk about it, that's ok too."

"It was so strange Lana, Father tried to tell me something at the dinner table. He was so agitated but he was able to say my name. He also said something else that has me puzzled. I think he was trying to tell me that I wasn't his daughter, and he said he hated me. Then he collapsed. He wasn't able to say anything else. I think that is when he had his second stroke. He wasn't aware of his surroundings from then on."

Mara hung her head, "I wanted him to explain the situation to me so bad; but all I could do was tell him what was in my heart." Tears spilled down her cheeks, "I told him I loved him, do you think he knew that Lana?"

"Yes sweetie, even if he could never allow himself to love you back, he knew you loved him."

Mara took a tentative bite from her roll and washed it down with a big gulp of milk. "I don't think he was aware that we were there, but I bared my heart to him just the same."

"Mara, you will be a better person for getting that off your chest. It doesn't matter if your Father heard you, the main thing is you were able to speak the words that you've held back for so long."

Mara let loose with all the pent up feelings and emotions she had kept inside her for 26 years. She cried for the lost opportunities and for the Father she never had. She cried until no more tears came, while Lana stood beside her stroking her forehead.

She quieted; all she could hear was the furnace kicking on. Lana said nothing. Mara thought she probably knew her whole story but would not violate the confidentiality of friendship to tell her.

Her cell phone rang breaking the silence and she reached to pull it out of her purse.

"Hello."

"Mara, this is Heather. I just wanted you to know that my Mom is coming right over to stay with Joe and the kids. I'll be there within the hour. Don't bother trying to tell me not to come. I know you, and you think you can handle this alone. You can't, and I'll be there with you to help you through this time." With those words the phone disconnected. Mara didn't have a chance to say a word. Well that's the way my best friend has always been, but I'm so happy she's coming.

The next phone call came in on the phone on the wall. It was the funeral home, just to let them know that all arrangements had been prepaid and prearranged and they didn't need to come in for anything. Mara told them she wanted the funeral held on Tuesday morning and visitation on Monday night. She knew that it would be better for her

Mother if the funeral and visitation happened soon. She was grateful she and her Mother wouldn't need to go to the funeral home. The funeral director would take care of the cemetery for them, Her Father's will had given specific directions for the funeral director and he would handle them. Her Mother had told her they had put everything in writing after her Father's first stroke.

The doorbell rang, and the first of the food began to arrive. They would have enough to eat for at least a week. With no family coming in, there would be too much. That was the small town way, you didn't suffer a loss without food brought to the family.

Lana stayed with her and checked often on Mara's Mother.

She came back from one of her trips and told Mara, "She's restless and I expect her to be getting up soon. She'll want to greet those that come over to express their condolences."

Mara nodded, she knew her Mother well enough to know appearances were important to her. She would feel she needed to live up to what her husband expected of her if he were alive. She had only known one way, and that was his way.

Her Mother woke up and after showering came into the living room. She looked tired and there were dark circles under her eyes. She was calm, and she remained calm throughout the evening.

Heather came and stayed with her until all of their guests had left. Being the only beauty operator in town meant that Barbara had many friends. Mara thought the whole town visited them and brought food. She knew she'd be able to freeze some food for her Mother to have in the days ahead. She wouldn't have an income until she opened her shop and tanning booth up again. Lana had left earlier to go home and prepare dinner for Bob and took some of the food to put into their refrigerator.

"Mara, what happened on Friday night?" Heather asked. "I know this happened so suddenly and was wondering what brought it on?"

Mara told her all that happened on Friday night. She told her everything her Father had said, and all the emotions that she'd gone through also. Finally, exhausted, she stopped talking.

It was time for Mara to rest. It had been a draining day, and the next few days would not be any better. She hadn't heard her cell phone ring, but when she went to bed, she found a message. It was from Carol telling her that Dean Hall wanted her to stay out for the full week. There wasn't anything pressing that needed done right now, and they would manage without her. She was grateful, it would allow her time to make sure her Mother was stable enough to stay alone. By then, her Mother would be itching to open the shop again and get on with business.

Chapter 36

The next day passed in a blur of visitors bringing food, phone calls, and murmured condolences. The visitation was from five to seven and the lines were long. The guest book filled with names would be the only way they would remember who had been there. John Conley had been a private man but well respected in the community. Barbara could count nearly the whole town as friends. A few of the people that Mara graduated with were also in line, as well as those she used to baby-sit. Jason's Mom and Dad came through with his sister. They expressed their condolences and she in turn expressed hers at the death of their son from cancer. They can say what they want about small towns, but they rally together when tragedy strikes for any members of the community, Mara thought.

The lines were gone and Mara and her Mother were alone. Barbara was swaying with exhaustion and Mara wanted to get her home to bed. Tomorrow would be another difficult day. Heather asked if they'd be all right by themselves and Mara assured her they'd be fine. They intended to unplug the phone and go to bed early. It worried Mara that her Mother hadn't eaten anything in the last few days. She intended to make sure she ate something before she went to bed.

The house was quiet when they returned home. Hope met them at the door, purring and rubbing against their legs. She was glad to see them and was ready for playing. They played with her, dangling a ball of string and tossing it for her to chase. They unplugged the phone and Mara turned off her cell phone. Tonight they only needed each other, and the little kitten to cheer and amuse them.

At least Mother ate something before she went to bed, she will need the strength for tomorrow. Mara, picked up in the living room, and put the dishes in the dishwasher. She wanted to get up to a tidy home. The Minister at the Church her Mother and Father attended was handling the funeral, and a friend of her Mother's was going to sing a couple of her Father's favorite hymns. She locked the doors, turned out the lights and went to her room. She looked around, the other night she had been too tired to realize everything was the same as it was when she left on graduation night. Her diploma and tassel were lying on the dresser; the posters of her favorite rock stars were still on the walls. She opened her closet and found the same clothes hanging there that had been there when she left. On a hook inside the door, she found her favorite flannel nightgown. It smelled fresh; did her Mother wash it every week just in the hope of her daughter coming home? She must have, the rest of the clothes didn't smell so sweet. She took it off the hook and slipped it on. She felt 18 again, but no, not really. She had come too far and learned too much to be the same 18-year-old young woman she had been the night she graduated.

The room was the same, but the woman within her was different. She was now a woman, with a mind and opinions of her own. She now knew she couldn't make her parents happy, but she had the responsibility to be happy from within her own soul. Yes, she had changed but her resolve was still there. She would find out about her past and know the reason her Father had looked at her with loathing in his eyes and had shrunk from her touch. The truth would come out; she just had to be patient until her Mother was willing to open to her.

She tossed and turned on the single bed. Tonight the memories were keeping her from going to sleep. She thought of the many nights she had listened to her parents having 'discussions', they were too civilized for arguments. At least that's what her Mother had told her when she asked the next morning. She thought of the many times she heard her Mother and Father's steps going down the hall to their room. The times her Father's had hesitated just outside her door, and how she prayed he'd just come in one time to kiss her good night. She remembered the times she considered climbing out the window and making an escape. She had wanted to run away since she was 12 years old. She thought of the times this room had been her safe haven, when she felt everyone in the world disliked her, she could come here and read the same books that were still on her bookshelf tonight.

She remembered the few times her Mother would come into the room and read to her. It was always on a night when her Father was attending a Church meeting. This room had also been her prison, banished from his sight for days on end for some infraction she had unwittingly committed. Her Mother would bring her meals to her, but would not speak. She was in total isolation. During those times, she lived in a pretend world. Her own world where she was a princess and both parents loved her. They were always at her school, helping with homework, and watching her play practice. They stood with their arms around her in the same pew they always sat in when they went to Church. She had been so sure God couldn't love her, after all, her own Father didn't. She knew better now, but even after all these years had passed, it still hurt. She had always looked for a Father figure in her life; unfortunately, her one relationship had been with an older man that reminded her of her own Father. She had remained in the situation even though she knew it was unhealthy. She didn't want to believe that she could be a failure again. Only with the help of her counselor was she able to break away from him and turn her life around. She was careful to make sure she wasn't falling into the same traps and the same way of life she had always known. It was hard, but it was worth the effort. The same recurring dream assailed her when sleep came. It was always the same, and nothing new this time to give her insight to what it meant.

Chapter 37

The day her Father was buried was raw and blustery. Winter had arrived in the Midwest and chilled Mara to the bone. Frost covered her window and she could feel a slight breeze coming because the storm window was still up. She jumped up to close it, her bare feet tingling on the hardwood floor. She hadn't slept well, but she'd make it through the day. She had to, for her Mother's sake. She heard voices and knew Lana had arrived; she could smell the coffee waiting for her. She grabbed her robe and slippers and went downstairs. Lana had heard her stirring and a cup of coffee was sitting on the table as well as a piece of fresh coffee cake. Her Mother looked tired, but determined this morning. Mara knew she would be strong. It was her Mother's way. Only later would her feelings come out. Mara wanted to be there for her when they did.

Her Mother had already showered and dressed in the clothes she was wearing to the funeral. The phones were still off so the morning was quiet. The three women sat drinking their coffee and talking over the coming day. There would be a dinner at the Church after the service, and then it would be over. A ten o'clock service would allow them to come home in the afternoon and be alone.

Mara finished her light breakfast and went back to her room to shower and change. She knew she didn't have a black dress, but she did have a navy blue one. She thought it would pass inspection. She applied what little make up she used and was ready to leave. Hope was sitting on her bed with watchful eyes. She sat down for a moment and stroked her long fur. Hope looked like a different kitten, with fur brushed and her body plumper with regular feedings.

"Hope, you stay home and wait for us, we will be back and we'll need your purrs and loving ways. You'll have your choice of which lap you want to curl up in, it doesn't matter which, and we'll both welcome your company." She stood up, took one last look in the mirror, and left the room.

The family car from the funeral home was waiting at the curb. Lana and Bob were riding with them. Mara was glad they'd have someone in the car with them. She didn't know what to say to her Mother, and didn't want to have only silence between them. As expected, Lana talked and soothed them as they went to the funeral home.

The funeral director requested they come early. They went to have one last look at the man who had been a part of their lives and now was no longer with them. Barbara touched his hand, the one with the wedding band. Lost in her own thoughts she stood near the coffin for several minutes. Then it was Mara's turn. She stood there looking at the face that had not once smiled at her. She'd said all she wanted to say to him that night at the hospital, she didn't touch him. She thought in horror that he might even in death, recoil from her touch. Rest in peace Father and know that I love and forgive you.

After closing the coffin, the blanket of roses that had streamers saying 'Father and Husband' sat on the coffin. Mara and her Mother sat down in the second row. There was a family section reserved but only two people would occupy it. There was no one left to mourn. The room began to fill as soft organ music poured out of the speakers. They heard whispers and shuffling of feet. Several times someone would come up behind them to lay a hand on their shoulder or to lean down to whisper their condolences.

There were a few flowers, more plants because anyone who knew her Mother knew that she would rather have a live plant than cut flowers any day. She adored them and they thrived under her care. I won't have to buy any plants for my apartment now, she thought.

The man who had been Pastor to her Father gave the eulogy. The room was silent with no sobbing heard. He had been an aloof man with few friends. The ones that were there were her Mother's friends. He kept his private life, private. Tears stung Mara's eyes as the hymns filled the room. Amazing Grace had always been her favorite as well. She felt the song belonged to her alone. Especially the line that said 'saved a wretch like me' she felt it was God's way of telling her He loved her if no one else did.

It was over, the friends filed out and left Mara and her Mother alone with the coffin. There would be a few words at the cemetery but this would be their good-bye. Barbara bent down and whispered "wait for me, I'll come to you someday." Mara again had no words to say, all she could do was lay her hand on the coffin bid the man she had known as Father good-bye.

They wheeled the coffin out to the hearse as Mara and her Mother walked to the family car where Bob and Lana waited for them. They snaked around town to Riverside cemetery. With little fanfare, the funeral ended and the small group left to have lunch together in the Church's fellowship hall. That too was soon over. The family car was waiting to take them back to the house. They invited Lana and Bob to come in with them, but they said they needed to go home. They went across the yard and let themselves in their front door.

Mara unlocked the door and sure enough, there was Hope waiting at the foot of the stairs to welcome them home. Her purring resounded throughout the small foyer. She brushed against their legs winding around and around them, first one then the other. The soft fur felt so comforting, they both reached down to pet the little kitten that had so much love to give. Mara's Mother stretched out on the couch, and Mara chose the lounge chair.

"I'm glad it's all over," said her Mother. At the end, he was difficult to live with. I loved him with all my heart, but it was tiring." Mara didn't know what to say. Her Mother hadn't ever been this open to her. She wanted so much to ask the questions that were burning in her heart and mind. She waited eagerly, but her Mother had drifted off to sleep. She needs her rest; I'll talk to her tomorrow. She went to the linen closet, picked one of the extra blankets, and draped it over her Mother's sleeping form. She leaned over and kissed her on the cheek. Good night Mother, I love you.

Chapter 38

The next morning she awoke with no one in the kitchen and her Mother still sleeping peacefully on the couch. Hope was nestled behind her curled legs. Her Mother looked peaceful, this would be the beginning of a new way of life for her. She tiptoed out to make coffee and start fixing breakfast. She was hungry today; she wanted something that would stick with her. She decided she would fix bacon, eggs, and toast. It sounded good to her and she knew the frying bacon would have Hope stirring and her Mother waking up. She quietly opened cupboard doors and the refrigerator to get out what she needed to make breakfast. The day was gloomy again, and the thermometer on the back deck registered thirty degrees. She missed Heather and the fast moving tempo of their family kitchen. She imagined the fireplace burning, JJ getting ready to go to school, and Joe on the couch reading to Melody. She could see it all in her mind. She missed the atmosphere and love she felt in their home.

Soon the bacon was frying and she was whipping the eggs so they could have scrambled eggs. She had found some shredded cheese and scrambled eggs were her favorite and her specialty. Her Mother came into the kitchen, "Goodness Mara, why didn't you wake me up so I could go to bed? I slept in my clothes."

"Mother you were so tired, I didn't have the heart to make you get up. You needed your rest. You'll feel better after that good night's sleep."

Barbara sat down at the table while Mara poured her a cup of coffee. "Do you want me to warm the coffee cake in the microwave for you? We can have that with our bacon and eggs.

"Mmm sounds good to me, I think I'm hungry this morning. I don't remember eating much yesterday and I know we didn't eat anything when we came home."

Mara continued fixing the eggs and turned the bacon over. She knew her Mother liked her bacon done, but not too crisp. With the eggs nearly done, she took the coffee cake out of the fridge, put a couple of pieces on a plate and put them in the microwave. This felt good; it felt right to wait on her Mother today.

"Mother here's your eggs and bacon; I'll just get the coffee cake out of the micro and will warm up your coffee." Mara turned to put the plate in front of her Mother and noticed the tears spilling down her cheeks.

Her Mother said, "I don't deserve this kindness and caring from you. I've always loved you but never treated you as a daughter. I'm so sorry."

Mara knelt beside her Mother's chair and touched her arm. "Mother, you don't need to worry, I've always loved you and Daddy too. All that is in the past and we're a different family now. I forgave Father for the way he treated me, even though I didn't understand it. Please don't get upset about this."

"There are some things that you need to know. Events that happened long ago and now need to be out in the open. I can't live with the secrets any more. No one knows the whole story, not any one, just me. I have talked about some of the past with Lana but she doesn't have all the details. Just enough for her to give you extra love, to make up for what you weren't getting here at home."

"Lana told me I was not quite one year old when they moved in next door. She said she made my first birthday cake and brought it over to you because Father didn't wish to celebrate my first birthday."

"She's right, I am so ashamed of the way that I treated you at home. I tried to show you I loved you when you were with me in the shop. I hope you realized that Mara. I did and still do love you with all my heart. I just couldn't show it in front of your Father."

Mara hugged her Mother. "Let's eat our breakfast and put this off for a little longer. You need to eat, and I know you'll want to shower in case someone comes by."

Her Mother nodded her head and they bowed their heads to say a silent prayer. Mara ate like a hungry lumberjack. She didn't think she had ever felt so empty. She felt empty in both body and spirit, she knew she'd soon learn of her past, and now that it was here, it scared her to death.

They finished their breakfast and while her Mother showered, she cleaned the kitchen. She went to the utility room to clean out Hope's litter box and filled her water and food bowl. She purred and brushed against Mara's leg, she looked more filled out and sleeker; like a different kitten than the one she had brought home, was it only a week or so ago? So much had happened in such a short time. She felt like she had been through a hurricane. Frazzled and unsteady, she sat down in the lounge chair. She practiced her breathing techniques, imagined herself in her favorite place. Soon, feelings of anxiety passed and she was breathing normally again. She stayed in her beach scene for a little longer, just allowing the pleasant sensation of soft breezes and the smell of the ocean to soothe her.

"Mara, are you all right?" Her Mother asked while coming into the room.

"I'm fine; I learned this technique to calm down. I was in therapy for three years, and I learned to focus on my inner self and stop panic attacks. I also learned to focus on the positive and not the negative. It has been a huge help to me in the last few years. I feel I can walk with my head high and proud to be the woman I am. I found out it's ok not to be perfect. No one is, no matter what the media would have us think. No, I don't always avoid being negative or depressed all the time, but I know how to cope and understand why I am the way I am."

Her Mother looked at her and realized she was looking at a woman now, not the little girl she never took the time to know, or the teenager that had ran away. She was Mara, her daughter, and she knew it was time to tell her story. She deserved to know it was not anything she did that made her Father dislike her.

"Mara, let's have a quiet day today, then tonight when we're sure no one will be over, I have a story to tell you. What we can do is go into the attic and we'll talk over some happy memories I have. I want you to know about your birth."

Mara smiled, that sounded like a plan to her and she was enjoying the closeness that she was feeling with her Mother.

"Let me go shower and put on a pair of jeans and t-shirt," said Mara. "I can't wait to look in the attic. You said I might find some items to use in my apartment too."

Mara took her shower in record time, pulled her hair back into a clip in the back, and went downstairs to join her Mother. Barbara was sitting on the couch with Hope in her lap, looking calm and serene. Mara had heard that pets helped you to be calm, and she knew Hope was doing her part in keeping emotions on an even keel.

Chapter 39

They pulled down the trapdoor to the attic and climbed the stairs. Mara could tell no one had been up here for a longtime. They probably stopped using the attic when her Father could no longer climb the stairs. Her Father was the packrat, the saver of the family. Her Mother reached for the string attached to the light and pulled. The attic came alive, with light and memories. Mara stood there in silent amazement. Everything from my parent's marriage is right here. She felt like she was on a treasure hunt. Her Mother began poking around in boxes, brushing away spider webs, and dust balls.

"This will be the most recent stuff here. The farther back in the attic we go, the older everything becomes."

They started opening boxes. Mara realized that her Father had saved everything; every card he'd received was here in a box. Not one kitchen utensil went to the garbage, nor one magazine that had a historic headline on the front. It entranced Mara it was so much like opening a time capsule. She fell in love with several relics she found and put them aside to take home and decorate her apartment. Some were hurtful to see, the colored drawings that she had made at school, carefully tied together in a bundle in a box, labeled under something else in her Mother's neat handwriting. She found kitchen appliances that she'd be able to use in her apartment and set those aside. It was like looking on her parent's marriage from the present to the past. She couldn't wait to get to the next box. Her Mother would sit at one box for a while and finger its contents, then sigh and go on to the next. The hours flew by. They stopped long enough for some lunch, and then went right back upstairs to go through more boxes. She began to get a picture of her Father that she never knew. He was in photo albums smiling and happy, there were several pictures of him and her Mother. Not too many of her with either of them. There were some school pictures, but no cute Kodak moments. No pictures of special events or birthdays.

"Why Mother, there aren't any pictures of me in any of these albums?"

"No, when you left he spent one whole day up here pulling out every picture he could find of you. He took them to the burn barrel and burned them. He thought it would make him feel better, but it didn't."

Tears slid down Mara's cheeks and she longed to begin questioning her Mother. She bit her tongue, she could wait, she knew in her Mother's time the story would unfold, and it wouldn't help to be impatient. She continued to open boxes and her Mother would exclaim each time she found something that brought back a happy memory.

They were getting toward the farthest reaches of the attic and Mara was beginning to find boxes labeled with her Mother's handwriting again. The labels read medical records, seldom-used recipes, or home cures. None of them had Mara's name on them; but inside was Mara's childhood. It was fascinating to see as each box unfolded its treasures. She didn't remember much of her childhood; she had obviously blocked it out because it was so unhappy. She picked up a rag doll and looked at it, she remembered this; she used to sleep with her every night. One time when her Father was punishing her for some small sin, he'd taken the doll away from her and she never saw it again.

"Oh Mother, please may I have that?" She said in a broken voice. I remember her, I named her Mary and I used to sleep with her every night."

"Of course, whatever you find up here is yours for the asking. I want you to have some memories of your childhood, even if it wasn't the best."

Mara clasped Mary to her breast and buried her face into the yarn hair. "I loved her so much and I told her everything each night before I went to sleep. I missed her so much when Father took her away, I wanted to die without her."

Mara gently laid the doll among the other treasures she had found, and knew Mary would sleep with her and again would listen to all of her secrets.

"Look Mara, here's your first Barbie doll. I bought it for you and gave it to you without your Father knowing about it. He didn't think it was good for a young girl to be playing at pretend dating. You used to play with her under the stairs, which was your secret place. You made clothes for her, and furniture, I thought you were creative. You'd pick up small items and smuggle them away, and I knew they were for your Barbie home."

Mara smiled, she remembered thinking of everything small that she could make into something for her Barbie home. She would confiscate pill bottles, and make them into stools for the kitchen. Boxes had become beds and blocks of wood had been appliances. She was happy when she was alone and playing with her Barbie. Every scrap of fabric became clothing for her Barbie. She remembered Lana had contributed a few items for her doll's home. A tiny feather she found in the yard had become a quill pen, and bits of paper turned into a writing pad. She had found a piece of vinyl tile from the new floor in the kitchen and it had been her Barbie's kitchen floor. Scraps from her Mother's sewing machine always found a place under the stairs, becoming rugs, or coverings for her bed and couch.

They found her Mother's marriage license and the album with their wedding pictures. They looked happy, there was no hint of the man that Mara had known as father. Her Mother cried when she opened one box, it was her wedding dress, fragile and yellow with age.

They opened another box and Mara caught a glimpse of what looked like a birth certificate. She knew it had to be hers. Her Mother picked it up and set it aside and upside down. "We will talk about this later tonight," she said.

A blanket covered it, but the toy looked new. She found a tiny rocking horse painted in bright colors with a jute tail. She could vaguely remember riding it as a toddler.

"Where did this come from?" She asked her Mother.

"Bob made the horse, he gave it to you for your first birthday. You loved it and would sit on it for hours. When you outgrew it, I almost died when I put it up here. I'm so glad it's still here. Obviously, your Father missed this when he was going through everything. You would smile so big when you were riding it, and you wanted to ride it even though you got too big for it. I loved watching you rock on it. You were always smiling and so happy. I could forget for a short time about the circumstances of your birth."

"I want to take that home with me Mother, someday I hope to have a child that can ride on it too."

Mara surprised herself when she said that. Children had never been part of her life's plan. She was reformatting her entire life, now she knew that marriage, and family life was not a bad thing. Maybe she would return Jerry Lowe's phone calls after all. He had called and left several messages with Heather.

Mara and her Mother, tired and dusty, decided to stop for the day. They went to their separate rooms and had a shower agreeing to warm up leftovers for their dinner. The refrigerator still had plenty from all the food that had been brought to them.

Chapter 40

Mara tidied the kitchen and took a shower. She and her Mother felt grimy and sweaty after going through all the boxes. The last box was one they didn't open. Barbara wanted to take it downstairs for them to open after dinner. She stared at it for a longtime, took a deep breath, and opened the box. Inside was a dainty christening gown. Carefully wrapped in fragile tissue paper a wedding picture appeared from the folds of the tiny gown. The picture was wonderful, picturing a happy couple. They looked nothing like the parents she had known as a child.

"I took you to Springfield to have you christened. Mara, this is my story and I've wanted to tell you, but your Father was a proud man and he didn't want you or anyone to know the truth. We loved each other so much at 20 years old. I finished cosmetology school, and John had a good job at the plant. We enjoyed being with each other. He helped me to set my shop up and was as excited as I was the day I had my first customer. We decided to make our life complete and try to have a child. We tried and tried for over five years but nothing happened. I had all the tests and they came back fine. It took me two years to talk John into having similar tests. When he learned he was sterile, it devastated him. We'd never have a child together."

Mara gasped "But Mother?"

"No Mara, please let me tell it all, or I might not be able to finish the story that you deserve to hear."

Mara sat back in the chair and continued to listen. Her questions would wait for now.

"We were both so upset, and he would have nothing to do with adoption. It was going to be his child or no child. I didn't care; I knew that I had a lot of love to give to a child. I looked into foster care but John wouldn't hear of it. He changed after that; he started reading the Bible, waiting for the Lord to show where he had sinned. He pored over the Bible, went to every meeting they had at the Church. It got to the point that he was gone nearly every night of the week. We weren't talking, communicating, and were drifting farther and farther apart. We didn't talk about it, he was too proud. Instead of mellowing, as he got older, he became more hardheaded and set in his ways. He quoted Bible verses endlessly and the Church and the work that he was doing there was the number one priority in his life."

Barbara stopped, took a sip of tea, and started in again. "One night, he was going to a board meeting that I knew would last until at least 10. I decided to go to Decatur and shop at the mall. A favorite client had a birthday coming up and I wanted to find something she had mentioned seeing earlier that week. I ended walking the mall back and forth, even though I had already picked up the gift for my friend. I window-shopped, tortured myself by going into the baby departments and lingering over all those cute little outfits for tiny babies.

As I was walking, I noticed this man with the most piercing green eyes I had ever seen. It seemed like every time I looked in a store window he was behind me. I tried to dodge him a couple of times, but he looked harmless, so I let him stare and didn't worry about him. I know I should have been more careful, but I was enjoying my time in the mall and just didn't give him much thought. I stayed longer then I intended to, but I knew John wouldn't be home for another hour or two. I gathered my packages, picked up something to drink at the pretzel shop, and prepared to go home. I'd parked in the back, the mall was having a craft show that weekend, and the parking lot was full where I would normally park. I parked behind Penney's near the garage area. I didn't realize it wasn't as well lit as the rest of parking lot. Its use was mostly in the daytime for cars that were waiting for repair.

I walked out alone with no sense of warning or apprehension. I was happy I'd found the present for my friend and had walked off some tension. At home, I felt as if I were walking on eggshells all the time.

I didn't hear a sound, but when I got to my car, someone grabbed me from behind. I fought, tried to scratch him with my keys but he was strong, he put his hand over my mouth so I couldn't scream, then he shoved me into the backseat of my own car.

I couldn't do anything; he kept his hand over my mouth. He kept talking to me as if I wanted to hear him talking. The only sight I remembered after the assault was those beautiful green eyes. I was crying, and he told me to shut up, he didn't hurt me, but he did. I never had a chance to recover from the physical hurt and the emotion battering. I didn't know what to do, so I went home to wait for John to come home. He was my rock, he would tell me what I needed to do.

I got home and took a hot shower, scrubbing my skin until I felt it was raw. All I wanted was to get rid of the feel of his hands all over my body and the taste of his palm on my mouth. I scrubbed, scrubbed, then sat under the shower spray, and cried. That's where John found me when he came home that night. He dragged me out of the shower and dried me off, putting me in a nightgown and robe. I was shivering so hard; he wrapped a blanket around me and took me to sit in the chair. He went to the kitchen and brewed me a cup of tea. I could hardly hold it in my hand; he had to guide it to my lips.

Then he knelt by the chair and I told him what happened. He was furious, but at me. Why didn't I park in a safer place, why didn't I tell a security officer what was happening? It all ended up being my fault. He said no one must ever know. He'd lose his position on the board at Church and we'd be the talk of the town. He convinced me to put it out of my head and get over it. I had to agree, he was the absolute ruler of the household by then. I didn't have a chance to do anything but agree never to tell anyone what happened. He told me the chance of catching the rapist was small, and we didn't need to be the brunt of all the gossip. I went along with it, I was too young to know what to do, and I didn't want to go against his wishes. I still wanted to make him happy and have a life together again.

Chapter 41

Six weeks later, I found out I was pregnant. He ranted and raved for days. He tried to convince me to have an abortion, but I stood my ground on that. I knew this baby was still a part of me and I wanted it. He tried for weeks to talk me into it. I think it was the first time in our marriage I stood up to him, I would win this battle. So, I made plans to keep the baby. He grudgingly agreed to raise the baby; his standing in the community was his prime concern. He didn't worry about me, just how it would look to the rest of the town. We'd kept it a secret when we discovered John was sterile, so it was easy to pass you off as his child. Already considered the town grouch, no one thought it unusual when he didn't enjoy the attention. We kept everything low-key, and he made no effort to help get a room ready or to assemble clothes for you. I thought he would change once you arrived, but I was wrong again. He made me feel I was dirty and I was the one to blame, and he would have nothing to do with you at all. He made it clear to me from the beginning that you would be his daughter in name only. He kept his word. I thought he would change once you arrived, but that didn't happen. You were so adorable and smiled all the time, but nothing would break the ice that surrounded his heart. Sometimes, I thought I would see him soften, but then in the next moment, he hardened his heart and you were just an annoyance he had to bear. I'm sorry Mara, I know this is hard for you to hear but after all this time, I knew I had to tell you the truth."

"Did they ever find the man?"

Mother and daughter met in the middle of the room, hugging and crying. A new relationship would start tonight. A relationship both of them had longed for all of Mara's life. She finally understood why her Father treated her as he did. It didn't stop the hurt, but at least she knew the truth. She would begin dealing with it all when she was able to absorb it. She was strong, she knew she could do it, and now she had a new and better understanding with her Mother. She was happy that God had given her this chance. She was glad she had forgiven and told the man she had thought was her Father that she loved him. She knew she'd done what she had to. She felt at peace. This is what she came home for; she'd have to deal with the fact her Father never loved her. She knew she could. She was not the same 18-year-old young woman that had run away from this unhappy household.

"Mara, I am so tired, if you have any questions, could we please go over them tomorrow. I need to go to bed."

"Of course Mother, I don't think I have any questions, and I don't want to open any more old wounds for you. I know my questions can wait. I know what I need to know for now."

Both women again hugged each other and went to their separate rooms. Mara laid awake for some time, before she drifted off in a restless sleep. She was sure her Mother was having a hard time sleeping as well. We can make it, I'll get my

Mother help as well. She has lived with guilt for something that was not her fault, Mara thought.

She thought again of the dream that kept recurring to trouble her sleep. It was so close to reality, it was eerie. Thinking of her Mother torn between the love of her husband and the love for her daughter those many years, made Mara shudder. She hoped they would be able to be close to each other now. Her Mother would need the support and love that only Mara could give her. She had come home at the right time. It was divinely directed, of that she was sure.

Mara felt peace wash over her in waves. She soon fell asleep with no dreams troubling her that night.

"No, I never saw him again, but I thought of him every time I looked into your eyes. I read in the Decatur paper a few days later, someone else suffered the same experience as me. I felt it was my fault and I could have saved her going through the same ordeal, if I had reported it. He got away with it that time too. It could've been someone passing through. In one way, I was fortunate, he beat the other woman badly before he raped her."

Mara reflected, "My eyes, they're his eyes, that's probably where the eye disease came from. What a legacy, my unusual green eyes that everyone tells me are my best feature, and the disease that comes with it."

Barbara handed over the birth certificate. It had her name as the Mother, but in the space for the father's name the space was blank. "He wouldn't allow his name on the birth certificate. It was a difficult delivery and I was unconscious for a short time. When I woke up, he handed me this birth certificate. He had named you Mara. I was furious, he knew I was planning on calling you Catherine after my Mother."

"Why did he call me Mara?"

"He told me Mara is a name found in the book of Job in the Old Testament. It means 'bitter water'. He told me that every time he looked at you or thought about you, it was like tasting bitter water in his mouth. John was not a forgiving person. From that point on, we kept up appearances for John's sake. There'd be no divorce in his life either."

"Mara, I loved you. I couldn't show it around John. From the moment I first held you I knew one wrong move and our fragile marriage would crumble."

"Mother, you know it wasn't your fault. I love you and what you just told me doesn't change that. No, I don't understand why my Father could never accept me as his daughter, but in a way, I can too. Just knowing him for my 18 years, I knew his pride ruled him. He wanted nothing to upset his standing in the community."

"How can I ever make it up to you Mara? I am finally free to show you the love I've felt for you since you were a baby. Can you ever forgive me?"

Epilogue

It was Thanksgiving Day, snow had fallen the day before, and a blanket of snow covered the ground. Mara was on her way to pick up her Mother and going to Heather and Joe's for Thanksgiving Dinner. Heather insisted that they be there with her parents and others that didn't have a family in the area. She knew Mark and Tina would be there. They didn't have any family in the area and Heather insisted that Mara and her Mother come for dinner as well. Barbara had baked some pies and insisted on contributing her cherry, pineapple salad. The month had flown by. Her new job was giving her enormous satisfaction and felt pleased with what she had accomplished so far. She continued to spend a couple of weekends with her Mother and they drew even closer as the weeks went on.

Her Mother was ready when she arrived home, the house smelled heavenly with the smell of pumpkin pies filling the air.

"I'm ready Mara; I'll put foil around the pies. I have a pie carrier and the salad is in the fridge."

Mara looked at her Mother and noticed the change in her appearance. She looked younger and far less stressed then she'd ever seen her. She'd gone back to the shop where everyone who came in supported her with love and condolences. Lana and Jim visited every evening to make sure she was all right and to reassure her they were next-door, if she needed anything.

Cars already filled the driveway of the Davis home. They parked along the street and Mara helped her Mother with the pies and salad. Warmly welcomed at the door by Heather, they made their way to sit in the living room by the fire. She took the pies and the salad and handed them to Joe as he came around the corner.

"Hi Mara and Mrs. Conley, welcome to Thanksgiving dinner at the Davis house."

He looked great, and seemed to be in a happy mood eyes sparkling and a big smile on his face.

Heather took Mara aside, "Please don't be upset with me, but Jerry Lowe keeps calling for you. He's called and asked about you nearly every other day. He knew you wouldn't be ready for a call from him yet, but…well, I invited him for dinner today too. So please don't be mad, Ok? He's in the living room, go in, and say hello."

Ever the matchmaker, that's my Heather. Mara went into the living room and Jerry jumped up to lead her to a chair. Her heart jumped in her chest. Looking at him she thought, maybe there is a possibility I could have a normal life after all.

Dinner was a wonderful success, with everyone laughing and chatting. With dessert waiting in the kitchen, Heather stood and asked for everyone's attention. Joe rose and stood beside her with his arm around her waist.

"First, we want to thank everyone for all the help and love you have given us through the last few months. We couldn't have made it without your support and we want to thank you for it. We are happy also to have Mark and Tina here and we're thankful for answered prayers for them as well. Then we would like to announce, she took a deep breath, but Joe interrupted her blurting out "We're having another baby!"

They all stood and clapped and cheered, JJ said, "I'm having a baby brother."

"Well we don't know that yet son, but we'll soon see," Joe said giving him a hug.

Mara thought, a season of change for all of us. We have gone through so much in the past year. I'm so thankful I was here to be a part of it. She felt the love in the room, and looked over at Jerry, he was looking at her too. Their eyes met and held for several seconds. Yes, maybe I'll be looking for a different future also.

A quiet happiness stole over her spirit, it was the first time she could remember being happy with every part of her life. She wanted to keep this feeling in her heart forever.

###

The End